630L

Itch

**Donated
To The Library by**

Emily Bloedorn

McClure Junior High School

2010-11

Itch

MICHELLE D. KWASNEY

Henry Holt and Company
New York

Henry Holt and Company, LLC
Publishers since 1866
175 Fifth Avenue
New York, New York 10010
www.HenryHoltKids.com

Library of Congress Cataloging-in-Publication Data
Kwasney, Michelle D.
Itch / Michelle D. Kwasney.—1st ed.
p.   cm.
Summary: In 1968, after the death of her beloved Gramps, Delores "Itch"
Colchester and her grandmother move from Florida to an Ohio trailer park,
where she meets new people and, when she learns that a friend is being abused
by her mother, tries her best to emulate her plain-spoken grandfather.
ISBN 978-0-8050-8083-4
[1. Grandparents—Fiction.   2. Mothers—Fiction.   3. Child abuse—Fiction.
4. Friendship—Fiction.   5. Schools—Fiction.   6. Ohio—History—
20th century—Fiction.]   I. Title.
PZ7.K9757It 2008   [Fic]—dc22   2007027573

First edition—2008 / Designed by Patrick Collins
Printed in January 2010 in the United States of America
by R. R. Donnelley & Sons Company, Harrisonburg, Virginia

3 5 7 9 10 8 6 4 2

In loving memory of
Kathryn and Douglas Smith,
my *Gram and Gramps*

For
my editor,
Christy Ottaviano

Itch

Part One

Unjust

Unjust: marked by injustice; unfair.

I have liked that word ever since it appeared on our spelling list in second grade. Right after, I began noticing how often Brother Thompson used it in his Sunday sermons. "The sins of an unjust few imperil the masses!" he would shout, slapping his hand on the podium. And all thirty-seven of us—unless Widow Pickett was ailing, in which case there would be thirty-six—would lift our voices and exclaim, "Amen!" Beaver Creek Baptists were big on hollering amen.

Still, I spotted those unjust acts everywhere.

Take Mr. and Mrs. Winthrop, who owned half the town of Beaver Creek. Each Sunday morning they'd drop a measly quarter in the collection plate while my best friend Bailey Parncutt's mama and papa, who couldn't afford an indoor toilet, gave fifty cents. Or two-faced Lenny Potts, who acted like one of the twelve disciples during the service, then headed home to whip the daylights out of his son, Lenny Junior.

Gram tells me I shouldn't dwell on these thoughts—that the good Lord keeps tabs on everybody, and He'll dole out what's due when the time is right.

But Gramps understood me. He was just a kid when a bunch of angry white men torched the black town of Rosewood over a crime Gramps claimed a black man didn't even commit. He seldom met more than a few folks who agreed with him, but that didn't change his thinking any. Gramps had an opinion about everything—President Johnson, the Vietnam War, the sit-ins over in Alabama, you name it. When something wasn't right by him, he spoke his piece and paid the price.

I wished I could be more like him in that way. I have always been shy in the speaking-up department. My brain's a miniature thought factory, whizzing and whirring, kicking up notions like they're a dime a dozen. But opening my mouth and sending those thoughts on their way is a whole 'nother matter.

What if I sound stupid? I ask myself. Where'll I hide if people laugh?

One day I decided I would ask what the secret was. "Gramps," I said, "I've got a question for you," which was how most of our conversations started.

And he said, "What would that be, Itch?" Gramps had started calling me Itch four summers ago, following an especially bad case of poison ivy. In time, Gram took a hankering to it, as well. I didn't mind—not with a name like Delores.

"How do you do it?" I asked Gramps. "How do you say what's on your mind without worrying you'll rub folks the wrong way?"

He said, "I'd have to be a nincompoop not to worry. Speaking up takes courage."

"Courage," I repeated.

Gramps nodded. "Growing up helps, too."

I scratched my head. "Yeah? When's this growing up usually happen?"

"For you"—his chin puckered as he studied my face—"I'd say it's just around the corner."

Dang, if Gramps wasn't right.

Everything that followed from that moment onward was fixing to see to it I grew up. Except I'm not talking about gaining two inches in height or adding a shoe size, though both have happened since. I mean that other kind of growing up. The invisible stuff that happens inside your head, whispering so loud you can't miss it. Psssst. Don't look now, but you ain't a kid anymore.

But there I go, getting ahead of myself—something Gram claims I do altogether too often. I'll back it up—to the summer after I finished fifth grade and still believed there was nothing an orange Creamsicle and a ride in Gramps's Chevy couldn't cure. The summer Gramps died and Gram got the notion of moving us up north. The summer I met an almost-famous baton twirler named Gwendolyn who offered me a close-up look at *unjust*.

Yes, that's where I'll begin. At the beginning. Which was really an ending in disguise.

Melancholy

I remember every word of my final conversation with Gramps. That's because words are my specialty. I even keep a list of my favorites. Some I have chosen for how they sound, rolling off my tongue. *Whip-poor-will. Persnickety.* Others, like *omniscient* and *talisman*, I've picked on account of their meaning. But I *digress*—which is to say, I plumb near swerved off the topic.

Gramps and I were relaxing in the front seat of his Chevy Bel Air convertible. We were parked in the driveway, "watching the grass grow," as Gramps used to say. The top was down. He was puffing on an after-supper cigar.

I could hear Gram inside the house, sorting perm rods and disinfecting combs for her next day's appointments. Gramps—with the help of one of our neighbors, Leroy Garrison—had built Gram a beauty parlor in our garage. According to Gramps, Leroy was so dumb he could throw himself on the ground and miss, but he could hang Sheetrock faster than anybody. Together, they installed a head-washing sink, a chair with a dryer attached, and a styling station with a seat that lifted and lowered, depending on the height of the person Gram was looking to gussy up. Once Leroy asked Gramps what possessed him to give up his garage for a silly old hair salon. Moseying toward his Chevy, Gramps answered, "What you don't know about me, Leroy, is that I, myself, am part Bel Air and part tomcat. And neither one of them wants to be kept inside a dad-blasted house, now, do they?"

Gramps was always doing that—comparing people to things: car parts, animals, inanimate objects, some of them downright unseemly. Take Leroy, for instance. Gramps said he was equal parts flat tire and spent match.

That night, as Gramps and I sat in the driveway and the peepers called *reeet-reeet, reeeet-reeeet* back and forth across the buggy swamp and the scent of Gram's tea roses filled my nose with sweet smells, I became melancholy as all get-out. Then I got a strong hankering to talk about my mama.

Now, Gram didn't care much for the topic, seeing as my mama ran off ten months after I was born and was never to be seen or heard from again—except for a single postcard from the Grand Canyon that read: *Take good care of my baby girl. You're the best. I love you.* Then she signed her full name, Ruby Lee Colchester, with more curlicues than a ten-foot phone cord.

Gramps didn't mind discussing Mama, though. That night I said to him, "Gramps, I've got a question for you," just as I had ten trillion times before. Except I had no way of knowing there would never be a ten trillion and one.

Gramps clicked on the car radio. A Frank Sinatra song leapt from the dashboard. He puffed his cigar and asked, "What would that be, Itch?"

I stretched my legs out, staring down at my skinned-up

knees. "You know how you're always saying what folks are made of? Well, I was wondering . . ." I lowered my voice so Gram wouldn't hear me through the window. "What do you reckon my mama's made of?"

The upholstery crinkled as he sat back, thinking. "Your mama," he said finally, "is made up of equal parts of three things."

"Wait a second," I said. "How come everybody else you've ever told me about is made up of two things and my mama gets three?"

"Because your mama is a lot more complicated than most folks."

"I see," I said, though I wasn't sure I did.

"What's the best thing to use for catching fish?" Gramps asked me.

I squinted at him, sure this was a trick. We went fishing all the time. I could bait a hook in my sleep. "Why, worms, of course."

"Well," Gramps said, "your mama was one part worms."

I curled my lip up.

"Hang on. It's not like it sounds. Remember, worms ain't worms to a fisherman. They're bait. And your mama had plenty."

I felt myself blushing. "What's next?"

Gramps smiled. "Butterfly wings."

"Really? Why's that?"

"You seen pictures of your mama."

Indeed, I had. And though we were both born with the

same sandy hair and dark eyes, they looked a far cry better on her. "Yeah," I agreed, "she's pretty."

Gramps's smile faded. "But she never stayed put. She was just like a monarch, always flitting here and there. Only landing long enough for you to admire its beauty and say, 'C'mere and have a gander at this,' before it flew off."

The evening settled in around us. A band of pink, bright as cherry Kool-Aid, began to soak the sky. "The third thing . . . ?" I said, prompting Gramps, before he flitted off, too.

Gramps rocked his head back, staring into the dusk.

I waited and waited.

I decided to make sure he hadn't fallen asleep on me. He'd been known to spend the night in that front seat. "Gramps." I shook his arm. "You didn't tell me the third thing about my mama."

Gramps turned to face me, then slowly, sadly, he looked away. "I ain't figured it out yet."

Bob Dylan Was Right

"We're creatures of habit," Gram has always said.

To which Gramps would answer, "Oh, horsefeathers!" And sometimes, just to put her in a tailspin, he'd quote a Bob Dylan song she couldn't stand. "These times they are a-changin'," he'd sing—usually on his way out the door. Gram's a hefty package, so Gramps didn't cross her without an easy exit.

Gram liked counting on each day being prett' near the same as the one that went before it. But Bob Dylan was right, as we found out one fiercely hot morning.

The Fourth of July was only two days away. Gramps had tacked red, white, and blue bunting across the front of our house, Gram had been busy making salads since the morning before, and the Beaver Creek Fire Department promised their best and biggest fireworks display ever.

Gram drew her bath at seven A.M. sharp, just as she did every morning. Then she hollered out to Gramps, who'd spent the night in his Chevy, "Coffee's ready, old man!"

I glanced through the window at him. Gramps's fishing hat was tipped forward, shielding his eyes. He was bent sideways in what looked to be a mighty uncomfortable position. I thought, Surely he'll be asking Gram to rub his back with liniment oil.

The sun was already bright, melting everything it touched into blurry pools of color—like a box of Neapolitan ice cream left on the table too long. I hightailed it out the back door, heading straight for my wooden swing. It hung from a branch on our old yellow poinciana tree and had been home to so many thoughts I'd taken to calling it my Thinking Swing. Back in first grade, when Gramps made it for me, I'd ponder stuff like if I bit my nails (which I did), then chewed them up and swallowed them (which I also did), and I needed an emergency operation, would the doctor open me up and find a huge pile of nail dust inside?

My thoughts have changed a good deal since then. Take that particular morning, for instance—I was contemplating something Gramps had told me recently. "Life is like a recipe," he'd said. "If you got two basic ingredients—one, somebody to care about, who cares about you in return, and, two, a place to call home, no matter how humble—you'll be good to go." Now, Gram claims there is no such thing as coincidence, that everything happens on account of God's will. And if that's true, then God—at that very moment—was preparing to mess with my recipe.

I was just getting warmed up on my Thinking Swing when I noticed Bailey Parncutt starting across the backyard toward me. Bailey and I'd been best friends since the second grade, when her family moved to Florida from Virginia and our teacher paired us up for a science project. We soon discovered we were the only two girls in the class who weren't scared of handling the toads we were studying. Mary Stingpratt—who we later nicknamed Mary Stinkypants—said to Bailey, all nasty-like, "You shouldn't play with frogs, they'll pee on you and give you warts." After which Bailey thrust one hand—already spotted with several brown bumps—right underneath Mary's nose, saying, "How do you think I got these?" That shut Mary up fast. Bailey earned my immediate respect.

Bailey stopped a few feet from my swing. My toe bumped a low-hanging blossom, and yellow petals rained down around her. "Hey," she said, thrusting her hands in the pockets of her shorts. "Whatcha doin'?" Bailey knew full well what I was doing; this was just her usual greeting.

"Hey, yourself," I said back.

The sun reflected off the roof of Gramps's metal shed. The glare poked me in the eye, and I had to squint to see. When I realized Bailey looked upset, I jumped off my swing, landing square on both heels. "What's wrong?" I asked her.

Bailey dragged her toe through the burnt grass. "Nothin'."

"Nuh-uh." I knew Bailey too well. Something was definitely up.

She shrugged her shoulders. "My mama's gonna have another baby."

Bailey's huge family was crammed into a tiny two-bedroom bungalow. Her mama and daddy had one bedroom, Bailey and her three younger sisters shared the second, and the four boys slept on foldout cots in the living room.

"Oh," I said, forcing a smile.

"Her doctor thinks she's carryin' twins," she added, looking fit for tears.

Bailey wouldn't appreciate her eyes going all soggy on her, any more than I would if it were me. I reached for her hand and whirled her around. Then I let go. "Come on!" I yelled, taking off. "Last one to the swamp's a dirty, rotten egg!"

By the time we got through the woods, we were both out of breath. We collapsed against the fallen tree that straddled the gray-green water. Bailey had named that tree Annabelle after her ninety-two-year-old aunt. I'd never heard of any-body naming trees before. I liked that about Bailey; she had her own way of doing things. We shimmied across Annabelle till we reached the center of the bog. Jagged stumps poked out of the mire, like pencils snapped in two.

We sat there for the longest time. However far down that swamp water went, our silence went twice as deep. "I can help you babysit the twins," I said finally.

Bailey scratched a bug bite, digging till it bled. "Promise?"

"Sure." I nodded. "I'll teach 'em how to fish."

"But what if my mama has girls?"

I puffed my chest up. "I'm a girl. I fish."

"But what if my mama has sissy girls like Mary Stinky-pants?"

I stared out at the beaver dam, trying to think of what to say next. But my thoughts were interrupted by a long, loud scream.

"That's Gram!" I shouted.

I skedaddled off the log and through the thickets. Bailey was on my heels. When we reached the house, we hurried inside, searching every room. But there was no sign of Gram or Gramps.

I pushed open the screen door. It whined loudly—once for me, then a second time for Bailey—before walloping closed behind us. I raced toward the driveway. Toward the Bel Air. Toward Gramps, who was still sleeping. I told myself, Gramps never sleeps this late. But my heart didn't want to hear the words.

Gram was hunched over Gramps, cradling his head to her chest. His fishing hat was tipped back, and his face was milk white.

Gram held one hand out, stopping us.

"Wha—what is it?" I choked.

"Call for an ambulance!" she yelled.

"Why?" I yelled back. "What's wrong?"

Gram tipped her chin toward the house. "*Now,* Itch!"

I did what she said. I ran inside and picked up the receiver and dialed the operator. "We need an ambulance!" I shouted.

Bailey gripped my T-shirt sleeve, twisting it back and forth. "Do you think he'll be all right?" she whispered.

I couldn't answer her.

As I hung up the telephone, a new thought entered my mind. A thought that was strange and cold and unwelcome.

Because I knew. I just knew.

I'd never hear Gramps's voice again.

Cousin Effie's Letter

Gramps's doctor said he'd had a heart attack and that he'd likely died in his sleep, quickly and painlessly—a fact he said Gram should be thankful for.

Every man, woman, and child in Beaver Creek attended Gramps's funeral. Even though he wasn't the churchgoing type, folks knew who Orville Colchester was. In a town of a hundred and seventy-nine people, it's difficult *not* to know everybody.

Days passed in a slow, colorless blur. I felt far away from everything and everyone, including myself. I would glance down at my fingers as I ate my breakfast, wondering, Whose hand is that on my spoon? I'd watch it scoop up milk and cereal and start toward my mouth. Then I'd remember, Those fingers belong to the hand that belongs to the girl who doesn't have a grandpa anymore.

Bailey came by every morning after her chores were done. Each time she'd bring something different—the roller skates we'd strapped over our sneakers at least a hundred times; a bat, a ball, and a catcher's mitt borrowed from one of her brothers; an armload of Hardy Boys books she'd carried from the town library. But not much interested me.

She'd ask, "Whatcha feel like doing?" and I'd answer, "Nothing." We would stretch out on the crisp grass, loop our fingers behind our heads, and squint into the sun, sharing silence.

Then, four weeks to the day after Gramps passed, July 30, 1968, Gram received a letter.

Bailey had to leave early that day. Her mama had a doctor's appointment in Gainesville, and she needed Bailey to babysit. When I returned from seeing her off, Gram was parked on the davenport. It was time for her soap operas, but the TV set wasn't on.

"Gram?" I said, starting toward her.

I'd added *monumental* to my Favorite Words list a couple months back. And, although I had no idea who'd written Gram, or what they'd said, I could tell from the look on her face that letter was monumental.

Slowly, she looked up. "I heard from Cousin Effie. You remember her?"

I shook my head yes. Nobody could forget Cousin Effie. She was as wide as she was tall. Gram and her were inseparable—till last year when Cousin Effie married a Yankee and moved to Ohio to live in a trailer park, that is. I stared at the lined page. "What'd she have to say?"

"Effie heard about your grandpa's passing. She feels awful. She wants to"—Gram looked away—"to help if she can."

"Like how?" I asked. Unless she had some magic potion for bringing Gramps back from the beyond, there was no help in sight.

Gram tucked the letter in her apron pocket. She leaned on the end table to stand, and the wood groaned beneath her. "I'm gonna start dinner," she said, avoiding my eyes. "I think I'll make stuffed peppers. We haven't had them in a while."

I followed Gram to the kitchen. She opened the refrigerator, placed four bell peppers on the butcher block, and sliced each down the middle. "Gram," I asked, "what else did Cousin Effie say?"

She drew a long breath, then let it out. "One of Effie's neighbors, old Mrs. Tuttle, has been moved to a rest home.

Her family's put her place up for sale. Effie thinks it'd be the perfect size for—"

"Wait a minute! Is she suggesting we move to Ohio?"

Gram nodded.

"And live in a *trailer?*"

"A mobile home," she corrected me.

"You're gonna tell her no, right?"

Gram didn't answer.

I fell backwards into Gramps's captain's chair. I glanced around the kitchen—at the blue-checkered wallpaper Gramps had hung, at the cupboards he'd stained, at the shelves he'd built for Gram's knickknacks.

When Gram finally spoke, it didn't have a thing to do with the letter. "You know what I miss the most about your grandpa?" she said, pulling a chair out, sitting beside me. "I miss the little things. Like how his spoon clinked against his teacup when he stirred in the milk." She tipped her head toward the driveway. "Or how he smelled after sleeping in that dang car—like he'd rolled the night air up in his sleeves."

"I miss watching him nap," I said. "Every snore would get a little louder till he'd let out a rip-roaring one that woke him, and he'd bolt upright and shout, 'What the heck was that?'"

A smile tugged at the corners of Gram's mouth. But right after, as if she'd been caught doing something illegal, she stood, returned to the stove, and started breaking hamburger into her black iron skillet.

"We can't leave here," I told Gram.

She adjusted the flame beneath the meat. "Managing a house is a lot of work, Itch. Your grandpa tended to jobs I wouldn't know the first thing about. And I ain't got the money to hire somebody every time—"

"I can do plenty!" I interrupted. "I helped Gramps clean the gutters and mow the lawn and prune the rosebushes. I bet I could even change the oil on the Bel Air, I've seen him do it so many times."

The hamburger sizzled in the fry pan. Usually the smell made my mouth water. Not this time.

Gram washed her hands and shook them dry. "It ain't just the extra work."

"What do you mean?"

"I can't look at a single thing without thinking of your grandpa." She swallowed hard. "This house is filled with too many memories. I'll never get on with my life."

Her life. What about mine?

I stared at the shakers in the center of the table, thinking. Gram and Gramps went together like salt and pepper, and I'd never adjust to one without the other. "We can't just leave here 'cause it hurts," I told Gram.

"I'm sorry," she said. "But your grandpa's the one who left first."

Good-bye, Beaver Creek

Leroy Garrison hadn't set foot inside our house since he'd helped Gramps build Gram's beauty parlor. But there he stood, seven weeks after Gramps died, watching Gram count out one hundred dollars one ten-dollar bill at a time, pressing each against his wide, callused palm. The money was half of Leroy's payment for driving us—and all our belongings—to Ohio. "You'll get the rest of what you're owed when you get us there in one piece," Gram said sternly.

Leroy hooked a U-Haul to the hitch on Gramps's Bel Air, backing it across the lawn to our door. Gram had sold any furniture she considered unnecessary. According to her we were "paring down." According to me, we were leaving a three-bedroom ranch with a wide, sprawling yard for a stupid trailer set on a lot not much bigger than a recipe card.

The empty U-Haul glared at me—an open mouth, poised to swallow everything we owned. Leroy clomped back and forth, feeding it again and again till the whole house was empty.

I walked from room to room, saying my farewells.

Good-bye, kitchen. . . .

So long, living room. . . .

My voice echoed against the blank walls.

I saved the den for last. Gramps didn't like being cooped up inside. But when he did sit a spell, the den was his room of choice. The sun flooded in through the wide window. The knotty wood walls gleamed. I stared at the empty corner and pictured Gramps relaxing in his recliner, a book of crossword puzzles open across his chest, a snore rattling in his throat.

I swallowed hard. *Good-bye, den.*

I cut through the kitchen and out the side door, glancing across the yard at Gramps's shed. Gram had donated his tool collection to the Beaver Creek Baptist Church for their annual rummage sale—along with his clothes and shoes. She'd let me keep his fishing pole and tackle box, and a few other odds and ends. But everything else was gone.

A breeze blew and my Thinking Swing swayed. I hadn't been on it since the morning Gramps died. The notion of deep thinking didn't appeal to me.

Gram's voice thundered across the yard. "Itch? Bailey's here to see you." Gram paused, studying me like she was seeing somebody new. Maybe she was. Everything about me felt different.

I heard the U-Haul door slam closed.

I started for the front of the house, where Bailey was waiting, wearing a yellow shorts set I'd seen on her mama once before. She looked nice—dressed in that cheerful color, leaning against the turquoise fender of Gramps's car, our bushy green shrubs fanned out like a curtain behind her. As I stepped close, she held out a package about the size of a writing tablet, wrapped in the Sunday comics. "This is for you," Bailey said. It was Tuesday, the morning after her weekly bath night, and I could smell her strawberry shampoo. Strawberries were Bailey's favorite fruit, but they made her break out in hives. Each year on her birthday she asked for a bottle of scented shampoo so she could at least enjoy their smell.

I felt the edges of Bailey's present. "Is it one of your drawings?" I asked, hopeful. Bailey was the best artist I knew. She had stacks of sketches she'd made on the brown bags her mama saved from the grocery store. I was sure she'd be famous someday.

Bailey shrugged. "Guess you'll have to open it and see."

"Fair enough," I said, ripping the paper loose.

My whole body broke out in goose pimples. Pressed beneath the glass of a black photo frame was a drawing of my Thinking Swing. The picture looked so real I could smell the plump blossoms rising from the tree's gnarled branches. "Why'd you draw my swing?" I whispered.

Bailey squinted at me. "So you won't forget what matters. I'm gonna sketch something different every week and mail it to you. You can hang the pictures in your room, and before long Ohio'll look just as pretty as Beaver Creek."

"Fat chance of that," I muttered, fighting tears. "But, thanks."

Bailey held her arms out, and I walked straight into them.

She hugged me hard, rocking us both back and forth. We were sniffling and snorting and our snot was getting in each other's hair, but I didn't care. I was scared I'd never see my best friend again.

Gram reappeared, straightening the FOR SALE sign the real estate lady had stuck in the grass. She handed Bailey a shopping bag. "These are perishables from the icebox, Bailey. They won't last the trip. S'pose your mama can use them?"

Bailey forced a smile. "I reckon she can, ma'am. Thank you."

We piled into Gramps's Bel Air. Gram sat in the front beside Leroy, and I sat in the back by myself. Leroy turned the key in the ignition.

I leaned out the window. "I'll write to you," I called to Bailey.

"I'll write too," she called back.

Leroy stepped on the gas pedal and Gramps's car lurched forward. We clunked off the curb and bobbed down the street, the U-Haul fishtailing behind us.

Bailey stood at the foot of our driveway, clutching the paper sack, waving.

I strained my eyes as she got smaller and smaller.

Then, finally, there was nothing left to see.

Hello, Ohio

Whenever Gramps took Gram and me for a ride, his Chevy buzzed with constant chatter. Sometimes, he and Gram would scrap some. Gram always won their arguments. It's not that Gramps *let* her win—he simply didn't have a choice. Gram was the Boss. Once I asked Gramps what he reckoned Gram was made of. Without even pausing to think, he answered, "Brass tacks and cinder blocks." I screwed up my face. "But, Gramps," I said, "you're *married* to her. Ain't you supposed to say something romantic?" Gramps laughed so hard he nearly coughed his cigar across the yard. "A relationship's all about what you need, Itch. A loose cannon like me ain't got much need for orchids and foofaraw."

I clicked on my radio and turned the volume down low. Leroy had informed us he didn't like distractions, which was fine by me. It was bad enough seeing him drive Gramps's car. Watching him fiddle with the AM dial would have made matters that much worse.

The first day we drove as far as Nashville, and the following day we finished the trip. As we crossed the border from Kentucky into Ohio, Leroy called out, "Welcome to the Buckeye State!"

I glanced over my shoulder to see if what we were leaving looked any different from what we were coming up on. It didn't. "What the heck's a buckeye?" I asked.

Nobody had an answer.

There were nine trailers in the Lazy Acres Mobile Home Park, plunked at the foot of a long dirt road. By the time we reached that mishmash of mobile homes, Gramps's car was coated with a gray layer of grunge.

Gram studied the Polaroid picture Cousin Effie'd mailed. Pointing, she said, "There it is, Leroy. Number seven. The white one with the blue shutters."

Leroy parked on the wide patch of gravel in front.

One of my feet had fallen asleep. When I stepped out, pins prickled through my heel. I stretched, expecting the sun to greet me in its usual way—like huge, hot hands clamping down on my shoulders. But that Ohio sun barely said howdy. "What's today's date?" I asked Gram.

"August the twenty-first," she answered, gathering a sweater around her.

Dust hung in the air between us. I tasted it when I breathed. "Feels more like *December* the twenty-first," I grumbled.

Leroy scratched his ear. "You reckon that's 'cause Ohio's up north and Florida's down south?"

He was flat tire and spent match, all right. "Yeah," I answered him. "I reckon."

Cousin Effie appeared in the doorway of trailer number

eight. She bounced toward us, hollering, "Eunice! Delores!" With her bright orange shirt and missing front tooth, she reminded me of a Halloween jack-o'-lantern. First she hugged Gram, then me.

Tall, skinny Hollis was close behind. "I'll give you a hand," he told Leroy. They skedaddled around back, unbolting the U-Haul door.

Cousin Effie led the way toward our mobile home. She huffed up the steps and flipped the light switch inside. Straight ahead was a living room with two windows, a maroon rug, and brown paneled walls. To the right was a kitchen with a stove, refrigerator, and a matching washer and dryer. The two rooms didn't have a wall between them, just a counter. Everything smelled Pine-Sol clean.

"Hmm," Gram said. "Bigger than I imagined it'd be."

"That's 'cause it's a double-wide." Effie elbowed Gram. "I told you you'd like it." She started down a narrow hall, her hips brushing the walls on both sides. Pausing near the first door, she said, "I imagine this'd be your room, Delores."

I took a peek inside. A single window looked out on a spindly evergreen, a burn barrel, and a pile of overgrown bramble. I wasn't keen on the colors—white paneling and gray carpet—but at least the walls weren't pink. I hate pink. It was item number one on Bailey and my Things We Both Can't Stand list.

Cousin Effie took a few more steps. "This room's a tad larger, Eunice. You'd likely be comfortable in here."

The bathroom came next on the tour, followed by a tiny third bedroom at the far end of the hall. Gram nodded. "This'll be perfect for my ironing."

Leroy and Hollis emptied the U-Haul.

They assembled my bed in one corner and parked my bureau against the opposite wall. When they'd finished, I sat on the mattress, listening to the sounds drift in from the kitchen. Gram had a pot of coffee perking. Voices rose above the pops and sputters, and occasionally I would hear someone laugh.

Gram slid into conversations easily.

Not me. I was just the opposite.

I thought of something Gramps had told me. One day he reached in his pants pocket, removing a handful of coins. He spread all the pennies on the table between us, flipping them over so the Lincoln Memorial showed. "Itch," he said, "the human race is like a piggy bank, chock-full of pennies. Most of them are surrounded by other coins that look the same way they do." He separated two that didn't match. I squinted at the design on their backside. Instead of the Lincoln Memorial, twin stalks curved like parentheses around the words ONE CENT. "Those are wheat ears," Gramps said, pointing. "That's why they're called wheat pennies. They stopped making them in 1959, two years after you were born, so they're rare. But even rarer"—Gramps tapped a coin I was certain was a dime—"are the silver wheat pennies. They were only made in one year, 1943, 'cause our country needed the copper for the war. They're also the only coin you can pick up with a magnet. So you see"—his face grew serious—"those wheat pennies have to search a lot harder to find their own kind."

Reaching inside my duffel bag, I unrolled my dresser scarf, smoothing it across my bureau. On top of that I set my three favorite photographs—Gram and Gramps at a Fourth of July picnic; me and Bailey winning the potato sack race at the county fair; and Gramps assembling the bike he bought me for my sixth birthday.

I saw a nail poking out of the wall and hung my Thinking Swing drawing.

The kitchen chatter calmed. Effie excused herself to start supper. Hollis left to drive Leroy to the bus station for his trip back to Beaver Creek. Lucky Leroy.

Suddenly, the whole place was quiet. Too quiet, if there is such a thing.

I felt inside my bag for my clock. The time was off because the ticking had stopped. I turned it over and twirled the brass key, again and again, wishing you could do that with a person. Wind them up and set them ticking again.

Gram's feet padded down the hallway. She stopped in my doorway. "Settling in okay?"

I stared at my dresser. At Gramps's picture. "I s'pose."

Gram glanced around the room. "You got it fixed up nice."

"Thanks."

"Mind if I sit down?"

I shrugged. "Be my guest."

Gram sat on the edge of my bed. The box spring whined. "I know you ain't fond of my decision to leave Beaver Creek," she said, "any more than you're keen on moving to Ohio. But give it a chance, Itch." She fluffed my pillow, then leaned it against the headboard. "Nobody gets used to new surroundings all at once. Home don't happen overnight."

I didn't tell Gram what I was thinking—that my one and only home was a thousand miles away, where there were palm trees instead of evergreens and oceans instead of lakes, and you never felt cold when the sun was on duty.

But there was no point in saying this. Gram wouldn't understand. She was a regular penny, and I was a wheat penny.

When I looked up, I noticed Bailey's picture was hanging crooked. "Yes, ma'am," I said, standing to straighten the frame.

Gwendolyn

Days crawled by, slow as a slug in the hot summer sun.

Cousin Effie introduced us to our neighbors. The folks living in Lazy Acres weren't just lazy, they were old. Not that I had anything against old people—Gram was one—but

I was the one and only kid. And a bored kid, at that. So bored I actually looked forward to school starting.

I'd written Bailey three times, and I'd gotten two letters in return. She began both the same way—*Dear Delores, I miss you! I miss you! I miss you!*—and she enclosed a drawing with each. The first was of Annabelle, the swamp tree. The second was a sketch of our ranch house. The FOR SALE sign was crooked, the grass needed mowing, and the empty driveway looked forlorn, pining for the sight of Gramps's Chevy.

Now, I had been saving my allowance because there really wasn't anything to blow it on. But the day Bailey's second letter came I decided to spend some of that money on two new frames for her pictures.

Cousin Effie gave me directions to the Woolworth's store and drew me a map of downtown Lakeville. I knew I wouldn't need it. I was just like Gramps, born with a compass inside my head.

As I said before, Lazy Acres Mobile Home Park was plunked at the end of a long, unpaved road. When the milk truck came each morning I spotted the dust cloud its tires kicked up long before I heard its engine groan. So I took my sweet time moseying up that road. I was breaking in a new pair of white Keds Gram had bought me right before we left Florida and had no intention of ruining them with the likes of Ohio dirt.

When I got to the corner, I turned down Main Street, which would eventually lead me into town. The street was lined with sprawling two-story houses with wide hedges and matching close-cropped lawns. I'd added *pristine* to my Favorite Words list in fifth grade. And pristine could rightly describe those sidewalks. I didn't spot a single weed sprouting through the cracks.

I passed all the landmarks on Cousin Effie's map: the town library and the post office and the hardware store and the supermarket. Finally the downtown stores stretched before me. But Woolworth's was on hold for the moment. I was too busy gawking at a sight in the distance. Two traffic lights down, huge trucks lined both sides of the street. I hurried ahead, toward a wide open green. When I got there, clean out of breath, I read the large sign anchored above the front gate: STARTS TONIGHT! LAKEVILLE COUNTY FAIR!

My heart skipped a beat. Bailey and I never missed the county fair. The whole week before, we'd wear ourselves out doing whatever odd jobs Gram could drum up. We didn't rest till we'd earned enough money for a three-day pass.

I wandered through the gate, checking out the sights. Food tents were being raised, amusement rides assembled. A boy pounded a 4-H exhibit sign into the ground next to a long rectangular building. I walked to the window and peeked inside. Straw covered the dirt floor, and dust specks danced in the light beams. A pickup truck backed to the entrance and a lady unloaded caged hens. I thought of Bailey and how she'd crack me up imitating the rooster with the tuft of black feathers she'd nicknamed Elvis Presley.

Bailey would gather her hair forward and scratch her feet in the ground, clucking to the melody of "You Ain't Nothin' But a Hound Dog." I nearly soaked my britches laughing.

A pang of loneliness stabbed me, right between the ribs.

I started for the opposite end of the fairgrounds. Rows of benches faced a large outdoor stage. Above the platform, hundreds of tiny lights spelled out: HOME OF THE LAKEVILLE TALENT SHOW. I loved talent shows. I used to watch *The Ed Sullivan Show* with Gramps all the time.

I climbed the steps to the stage. An organ was parked in one corner and an emcee's stand in the other. Beyond that was a tall, skinny door. I snuck through it, down a narrow hallway backstage. Stage lights were labeled with colored tape. I peered behind a blue curtain, into a small, empty changing room.

A second set of stairs led to a grassy area behind the stage. Picnic tables were scattered between the trees. I headed toward the closest, figuring I'd take a load off my feet, when I heard a voice behind me say "Pssssst!"

I turned, startled. A girl about my age was crouched beside the steps. Her eyes were emerald green and her hair hung in blond sausage curls like Shirley Temple's. Red, white, and blue sequins were sewn in stripes across her long-sleeved leotard. White tights and blue dance slippers finished off her outfit. "Pssssst!" she said again.

I didn't know who she was talking to. I glanced around, but there was no one there. "Do you mean me?" I asked.

She rolled her eyes. "Do you see anybody else?"

I shrugged and walked toward her.

"I need your help," she said, turning her back to me. "Something's pinching me."

I moved her ringlets aside. "Your zipper's stuck on something." I tugged and pulled and jerked the tab, trying to see what it was. The girl was ten kinds of impatient, wiggling every which way. I kept saying, "Hang on . . . not quite . . . hold still . . . ," till finally I found the culprit—a thin blue thread tangled in the small metal teeth. I glided the zipper up its track. "There," I said. "All done."

"You're a lifesaver," she said, hurrying away. I watched as she climbed the steps, disappearing behind the dressing room curtain.

I was about to be on my way when the girl reappeared, carrying a shiny silver baton. Red, white, and blue tassels dangled off the round white ends. Bailey'd give her eye-teeth for a baton like that, but her mama said they cost too much. She made do with an old broom handle her father had sawed in half and spray-painted silver for her.

The girl bounded down the steps and across the grass. A tree spread its wide leafy branches overhead, dabbing shadows everywhere.

"What are you doing here?" I asked the girl.

"Practicing." She closed her eyes and stood very still.

"Okay, then," I said, turning to leave.

Her eyes flew open. "Wait!"

I did an about-face. "Wait for what?"

"Don't go yet." She motioned toward the picnic tables. "Sit down. Over there."

What the heck, I thought. Woolworth's isn't going anywhere. I did what she said.

The girl closed her eyes again. She pointed one toe forward and lifted both arms, holding her baton at an angle. Her chest rose and fell as she drew in a slow, measured breath. Letting it out, she sprang into action.

Her fingers were a blur as she spun the silver wand—in front of her, at her side, between her legs, in and out and around each knee. I held my breath as she tossed the baton in the air. It soared upward, higher and higher, spiraling in quick, perfect circles. Until it hit a branch.

The girl looked up, waiting for the baton to return. And it did, finally, slapping several branches before landing on the ground at her feet.

I clapped my hands. "That was great!"

She scowled as she bent for the baton. "That was terrible."

"No way," I argued.

"Yes way. A mistake like that would ruin a performance. And it only takes one. Then the audience forgets the ninety-nine good things you did before you messed up."

My, my. That girl sounded more like a grown-up than a kid. I glanced above her head, at the giant branch. I tried to think of how Gramps would explain such a mishap. "It was the tree's fault," I told her.

She batted her eyes. "What?"

"That tree plucked your baton out of thin air. I saw it with my own two eyes."

I could tell she was trying not to grin. "You did?"

I nodded, just like Gramps would've, heavy on the chin action. "Uh-huh."

She looked up at the tree, then back at me. "Well, if you saw it yourself—"

"Darn tootin'."

The girl's eyes narrowed. "You sound like you're from down South." She stood her baton on end, leaning on it like a cane. "Say something else."

"Something else."

"Ha, ha, very funny." She smiled. Her teeth were shiny and straight. "You know what I mean. Where do you live?"

While I'd been talking like Gramps, I felt confident. Now I was plain old me, and I felt suddenly shy. I stuffed my hands in the pockets of my cutoffs. "In Lakeville."

"I live in Lakeville, too. How come I haven't seen you in school?"

I shrugged. "School ain't started yet."

"No. *Last* year."

"We just moved here. From Beaver Creek." I wiggled my fingers in my pockets. They bumped into a half-finished roll of Necco Wafers. "Know where Beaver Creek is?"

The girl shook her head no.

"It's in Florida."

"Oh." She watched me unwrap the candies. "What grade are you going into?"

"Sixth," I answered, popping several wafers in my mouth.

"Me too." The girl stared. That's when I realized my manners were slipping. I tipped the roll toward her. Wouldn't it be just my luck—purple, my favorite, was next up.

"Thank you," she said, helping herself. *Pulverize* had been a fifth-grade spelling word. It didn't make my Favorite Words list, but I recalled it, all the same. If I had to use it in a sentence, I would say: That girl sure did pulverize those Necco Wafers.

The sunlight shifted overhead, squeezing past the last clump of branches.

I noticed a tall, thin lady in a yellow dress starting toward us. She walked with a limp, each step a kind of half glide, half hobble. "There you are!" she called to the girl. "Did you forget you have a hair appointment in fifteen minutes?"

"Shoot!" the girl snapped, swallowing with a large, loud glug. She swiped her teeth with her tongue and faced me, baring her pearly whites. "Quick. Check for me. Do you see any candy pieces?"

I surveyed her teeth. "No. Why?"

"My mother"—the girl nodded toward the woman— "she doesn't allow sweets." She reached for her baton case, then hoisted a navy blue bag over her shoulder. It booted her in the backside as she hurried away.

Halfway across the lot, the girl stopped. She whirled around and shouted, "I'm Gwendolyn, by the way."

"I'm Delores," I hollered back. "Are you in the talent show tonight?"

The girl didn't answer me. Her mother did, calling loudly, "Gwendolyn's *winning* the talent show tonight."

Yesterday, Today

I was so busy thinking about the county fair and meeting Gwendolyn, I plumb forgot about my plans. Partway home, I stuck my hands in my pockets and my fingers bumped into the dollar and two quarters Gram had given me to buy frames for Bailey's drawings. Actually, she hadn't *given* me the money. It was my allowance, raised a whole fifty cents on my last birthday, thanks to Gramps. Gram had disagreed with him, saying a buck fifty was too steep for an eleven-year-old. But somehow Gramps convinced her, and I am glad he did. By the time I finished my Saturday morning cleaning chores, I earned every single cent of that amount.

I recalled where I'd seen Woolworth's—three blocks back, just beyond a record store and a hair parlor. I spun around, pointing myself in the direction I'd come from.

My Keds clapped against the concrete. The sound

reminded me of Bailey and how we used to tape nickels to the bottoms of our sneakers, pretending we were tap dancers. I pictured her—arms waving at her sides, beaming an imaginary I'm Onstage smile as she tapped her heart out. Suddenly I missed her something awful.

When I passed the record store, the door was propped open, and a slow, sad song spilled out. I stopped, listening as a man sang about *yesterday*, when his troubles were few and somebody he cared for hadn't left him. I knew just how he felt. I'd return to yesterday in an instant if I could.

When the song ended I stepped inside the store. Beside the cash register was a phonograph. The arm bobbed back and forth as the needle wiggled in the last groove.

I thought of Gram's phonograph, which she'd placed on a stand beside her ironing board in the small third bedroom of our mobile home. Gram claims she can press laundry till the cows come home if Perry Como's crooning in the background. I'd never thought to ask Gram to use her record player. I'd never had a reason to. Till now.

A man walked past, shelving albums. He was wearing a tie-dyed T-shirt and wide bell-bottom jeans. His long gray hair was held back in a ponytail. I reckon he was what Gram would call a hippie. "Can I help you?" he asked me.

I said, "That song you just played, do you sell it here?"

He handed me a single black record. When I read the label—"Yesterday," by the Beatles—my arms broke out in goose pimples. I could still remember Gramps and me watching the Beatles perform on *The Ed Sullivan Show*.

When they sang "I Want to Hold Your Hand," Gram hollered in from the kitchen, "Turn that ruckus down!" She never fancied rock 'n' roll.

A fat lump crowded my throat. "H-How much for that record?" I choked out.

"All 45s are on sale today, in honor of my forty-fifth birthday"—the man smiled widely—"for forty-five cents."

Perfect, I thought. I can use two quarters for the record and still have a dollar left for frames. I counted out the coins on the counter. The man slid the 45 into a paper sleeve. He tucked it in a bag, along with my receipt and a red LAKEVILLE RECORDS pencil.

Outside, I took a left toward the hair salon. I recognized the stink of somebody getting a permanent wave. I was about to hurry on past when I noticed a HELP WANTED sign in the window. I thought of Gram and fished out my receipt, jotting down the phone number for her.

Inside the salon, someone waved. Now, I had added *mirage* to my Favorite Words list in third grade. It's a trick our eyes play, making us see things that aren't there. I knew three people in Lakeville—Gram and Effie, who were back at Lazy Acres making lemon pies, and Hollis, who didn't have enough hair to style—so I was surely seeing a mirage. Still, I had to be sure. I cupped my hands around my eyes, squinting through the glass.

Somebody was waving at me—Gwendolyn the baton twirler. She was sitting beneath a hair dryer, still dressed in her dance leotard, except she'd added a long, gauzy skirt to the getup. She moved her lips in wide, careful circles, mouthing something.

You should . . . I missed the middle part . . . *talent show tonight.*

When does it start? I mouthed back.

She screwed up her face. *What?*

I pointed at my watch. *What time?*

She held up seven fingers.

A door beside the hair-washing sinks opened and the girl's mother appeared, drying her hands on a towel. As I watched her limp toward Gwendolyn, a thought popped into my mind. I wondered what my mama and I would be doing together at that moment if she'd stuck around to see me grow up. A pain rose in my chest. Gram would blame it on gas, but this was a whole 'nother feeling.

I couldn't think of anything else to say. *Bye, Gwendolyn,* I mouthed.

She smiled slightly—what Gramps would call a feeble smile.

Her mother leaned close, tapping Gwendolyn's knee as she told her something.

Gwendolyn fiddled with a sequin, twisting and turning that shiny circle like she was fixing to rip it clean off. She didn't look up again.

Double Dose of Bad News

The mailman's truck was parked beside the boxes. I watched as he drove off, eclipsed in a dusty cloud, praying he'd left something from Bailey. Thankfully, he had. I tucked my picture frames and record under one arm so I would have both hands free. Carefully, I opened her envelope, unfolding a drawing of the Beaver Creek Grammar School. The windows were decorated with paper cutouts, and fall flowers filled the planters. The marquee spelled out: WELCOME BACK, STUDENTS! Except that sign wasn't welcoming *me* back.

Bailey's letter was written on notebook paper, just like her others. I ambled down the road, reading slowly, trying to make each word count. *Dear Delores,* she wrote.

> *I miss you! I miss you! I miss you!*
>
> *I only have a few minutes to write. Mama has an appointment with her baby doctor, and guess who gets to babysit?*
>
> *By the time you read this, I'll be back in school. I thought you'd like a picture to remind you of all the fun you're missing. (Ha! Ha!) We're going to have a new student. Her first name is Becky—just like the girl in* Tom Sawyer—*her last name is Montgomery,*

*and her family moved here from Atlanta. Her
mama sells Avon and lets Becky wear lipstick to
church. Last Sunday she had on a real pretty
color—pink as the inside of a conch shell. Just to be
neighborly, I told her how nice it looked. She said
she'd bring me a sample tube next week.*

"Lipstick?" I said, staring at Bailey's letter. "*Pink* lipstick?" To be sure I wasn't losing my marbles, I read the paragraph again. It still said the very same thing.

I let out a huff and crammed her letter in my pocket. When I readjusted my bags, I stabbed myself in the armpit with the picture frame. "Ow!" I said, walking fast, kicking every pebble in my path. "Ow! Ow! Ow!" Soon my new Keds weren't white anymore. But I didn't care. There was something about dirty sneakers and disappointing letters that just seemed to go hand in hand.

As I crossed our driveway, the theme song to *The Secret Storm* drifted through the screen door. I glanced at Gramps's Bel Air. Everything from road grime to tree sap to bird poop dulled its turquoise finish. I was about to continue on past when I noticed something out of the corner of my eye—a red and white FOR SALE sign tucked beneath a windshield wiper. I flew across the hood, whipping that sign free so fast I nearly took the wiper off with it. I stomped up the steps and burst inside.

Gram's eyes were glued to the TV. "Itch, there's cold cuts in the ice box if—"

"What's this?" I blurted out, shoving the sign forward.

She shot me a look, heavy on the eyebrows. "Can this wait till a commercial?"

I set my shopping bags on the coffee table. "No, ma'am. I reckon it can't."

Gram lifted the package of sugar wafers off the davenport, patting the empty spot beside her. I didn't feel much like sitting, but Gram agreeing to interrupt her soap opera was a miracle. So I sat, resting the sign on my knees—facedown, like hiding those terrible letters might make them disappear for good.

"Gram," I said, "why do you want to sell the Bel Air?"

"Itch, maintaining a car takes a lot of money. There's a registration fee and insurance and state tax." She paused, brushing cookie crumbs off the shelf her bosom made. "Besides, ain't nobody around here named Nelson Rockefeller, rich enough to cough up thirty-four cents a gallon for gasoline."

"But you've got Gramps's pension. And the money from the house, when it sells."

"When that house sells, it'll be used to pay what I still owe on *this*." Gram swept her arm across the room like she was showing off Emerald City instead of a stupid trailer.

I had to think of something fast. That car was all I had left of Gramps. "I know!" I shouted. "You can keep my allowance. That'll save you six bucks a month. I'll do all my chores for free, so you can use the money for the car. Whaddaya say?"

"Itch, even if I could afford taking care of that car—and I'm not saying for certain I can—it doesn't change the fact that your grandpa ain't here to drive it."

"*You* can drive it," I said. "You've got a license."

Gram harrumphed. "That license is from 1935, thirty-three dadblasted years ago. You think I paid Leroy Garrison two hundred dollars to drive us here 'cause I felt generous? No sirree. I haven't started a car since the day I married Orville. I wouldn't even know where the key goes."

I rolled my eyes. "In the ignition, of course."

"Don't roll your eyes at me, young lady."

I stared at the toes of my dirty Keds. "Sorry, ma'am."

Gram rested her hand on my knee. "Itch," she said, "keeping the Bel Air ain't gonna bring your grandpa back."

I jumped up, banged my knee on the coffee table, and hurried outside.

I threw the car door open and did a huge belly-flop across the back. Then I sat up, hugging Gramps's seat. It smelled just like him—equal parts cigar smoke and shaving cream and hair tonic. I mashed my face into the upholstery.

My throat burned and my eyes filled.

But I ain't a crybaby. And I had no plans of becoming one.

So I swallowed every sob.

Wake-up Call

I must've dozed off in the backseat of Gramps's Chevy. I woke to the crunch of driveway stone and rose slowly, rubbing sleep from my eyes. When something whapped against our trailer, startling me, I pushed the car door open.

"Hey!" a boy hollered, swerving his bike to miss me. He toppled to the ground, landing flat on his keister.

"Holy moly!" I hurried toward him. "I'm sorry. I didn't see you. Are you okay?"

The boy, who I guessed was the paper carrier, stood, brushing dirt off his behind. His red hair gleamed in the sun. Brown freckles dotted his nose, scattered like cinnamon flakes. He readjusted his canvas bag and told me, "I'm fine. Stuff like that happens all the time. I'm used to it. Last week a German shepherd chased me seven blocks."

"Sounds like a dangerous job," I said.

"It can be." He tipped his chin toward our trailer. "You live here now?"

"Yeah. My grandma and me."

"The lady who used to be here—Mrs. Tuttle—did she croak or something?"

"I think she moved to a special home for old people."

"That's too bad. Mrs. Tuttle was a real good tipper. She

gave me a buck a month. Except her eyes were failin' her, so sometimes she'd give me a five by mistake." He squinted at a car starting down the dirt road. "How's your grandma's eyes?"

"Twenty-twenty."

"Oh, well." He waved a bug away. "Least she ain't got any dogs."

I don't usually smile at people right off the bat. Gramps taught me, "First time, nod; second time, listen; third time— if there is a third time—then you can let 'em see you smile." But I couldn't help myself. A wide grin spread clean across my face.

The paperboy smiled, too. Then he bent to pick up his bike, swung his leg over the seat, and pedaled off.

I snatched the *Lakeville Gazette* off the step on my way back inside. Large headlines sprawled across the front page: COUNTY FAIR STARTS TONIGHT! There was a close-up picture of a kid eating cotton candy, midway lights twinkling behind him. With all the goings-on about Gramps's car, I'd forgotten about the fair. I checked my watch. It was already five o'clock, meaning Gram would serve dinner any minute. And the talent show would start in two hours.

The television was on, warming up for the evening news.

Gram stood before the stove, heating a saucepan of Cousin Effie's black bean and ham hock soup. The walls in those dern mobile homes were so thin I'd listened to Hollis pass gas since his first serving two days ago.

I set the newspaper on the counter. I told her, "The county fair's this weekend. There's a talent show tonight. When I went to the store earlier, I met a girl who's gonna be in it. A baton twirler named Gwendolyn. I watched her practice. She's really good."

Gram dipped her ladle in the soup, tasting it. She made a face and added salt.

"If it's all right," I said, "I was thinking maybe I could see her perform."

"What time's the show?" Gram asked.

"Seven."

Gram wiped her hands on her apron. She reached into the cupboards, handing me two large bowls, my cue to set the table. "Not this time, Itch."

"But why not?"

"I'm sure that show's gonna last awhile. I don't want you out after dark, not yet."

"But Gram, I've got this place figured out top to bottom."

"No means no, Itch."

I tapped my chin, thinking. "I know. *You* could come with me."

Gram harrumphed. "Now, what am I gonna do at a county fair talent show?"

My answer was downright mean. I couldn't help myself. I was still sore about the Bel Air. I spit out, "If Gramps was here, *he'd* take me."

Gram was motionless, like somebody had tapped her in freeze tag. When she finally moved again, she breathed a hard sigh. Then she dipped the ladle in the pot, scooping soup into both our bowls. Almost like nothing had happened.

The news came on, reporting the latest deaths in Vietnam.

I reached for my milk glass and swallowed several times. But I couldn't wash away the knot lodged in my throat. "I'm sorry," I said, "I shouldn't have said that. I—"

"Now, now." Gram raised her hand to shush me. "Sit yourself down and say grace. We ain't got time for chatter if we're gonna make it to the fair before the show starts."

Twirling with Fire

Five minutes before showtime, Gram and I reached the front gate.

We elbowed our way toward the outdoor stage. We'd barely plunked our behinds on a bench when a man in a gray suit breezed across the stage. "Good evening!" he announced. "I'm Jay Valentine, your host for tonight's show. I'll be presenting twelve talented acts, but only one performer will be chosen to claim the 1968 Lakeville Talent

Show trophy." He motioned toward a marble and gold statuette. Everyone gasped, and right well they should. That trophy was huge.

The first act was a ventriloquist, followed by a barbershop quartet and a boy who juggled oranges. A clarinet player came next, then a ballerina and a country-western singer. I was itching in my britches, eager for Gwendolyn's turn. By the time the eleventh act finished, the night air had grown chilly. As the sun set behind the stage, Jay Valentine announced, "Our last performer is an eleven-year-old baton twirler, Lakeville's own Gwendolyn Parish."

"That's her," I whispered to Gram.

The stage lights dimmed. Midway sounds clattered in the distance.

When a spotlight blinked on, Gwendolyn stood motionless in its center. Her head was bowed, her hair arranged on top in a cluster of tight blond curls. Her hands were poised at her sides, a baton in each. She didn't move a muscle till music boomed through the sound system—patriotic music, like you'd hear at a Memorial Day parade—then she sprang into action.

I gripped the edge of my seat, watching Gwendolyn glide across the stage. Dancing. Spinning. Twirling. The things I'd seen her practice earlier were nothing compared to what she performed now. I was breathless.

"She's good," Gram said, tapping her foot to the music.

"She's ebullient," I added. *Ebullient* had been a fifth-grade spelling word I'd never had the opportunity to use. Till now.

"Ebullient?" Gram repeated. "Pretty highfalutin' word. What's it mean?"

I was afraid I might miss something. "Lively," I whispered quickly. "Bubbly."

Abruptly, Gwendolyn stopped, tipping her batons toward the stars. She crossed the stage, bending before an open trunk. I tried to make out what she was doing, but I couldn't. Not till I saw a small flame. Then a second, and a third, and a fourth.

"My Lord," Gram gasped. "She's setting those baton tips on fire."

Gwendolyn returned to the spotlight. The red-orange tongues lapped at the black sky. The sequins on her costume gleamed like a million tiny sparks. Over the loudspeaker a new song played—slow and mysterious, music a snake charmer would use. Gwendolyn twirled the fiery wands at her sides, then over her head. She wove them in and out between her legs.

I watched as the first baton soared upwards, followed by the second—higher and higher, until they seemed to pause midair, pirouetting far above her head.

Then, slowly, they both began to fall. I thought of what had happened earlier—how the tree limb had gotten in her way and the baton had slapped through the branches.

A mistake like that would ruin a performance. . . .

I craned my neck. The fiery wands pinwheeled through the darkness. The audience roared as the first baton landed in Gwendolyn's outstretched hand. Then the second.

Gwendolyn took a bow. She returned her batons to the trunk, and the flames disappeared. Then she disappeared.

Moments later, the lights flickered on. Jay Valentine called the performers onstage. He dragged the trophy to the center and tore the flap on an envelope. "I am pleased to announce the judges have unanimously declared that the winner of the 1968 Lakeville Talent Show is"—he paused—"Gwendolyn Parish!"

Gwendolyn waved at the audience. People crowded toward her, snapping pictures. Jay Valentine thanked everyone for coming.

Gram squeezed my arm. "Don't go far. I need to visit the bathroom."

"Okay," I said. "I'm gonna congratulate Gwendolyn."

I waited by the back steps as the performers trickled out, dressed in their regular clothes. Gwendolyn appeared, still wearing her costume, slipping a poncho over her top. When she saw me, she hurried down the stairs. "Did you catch the show?" she asked. With her red lipstick and blue eye shadow, she looked more like a teenager than a kid.

"Yeah, I did. Congratulations. That's some trophy you won."

"I know. It's gigantic. I'm running out of places to put them all."

"What do you mean?"

She unsnapped her clip-on earrings. "I've got five more just like it."

"Are you saying you won the Lakeville Talent Show five times already?"

"Six, actually, counting tonight."

A small boy stopped beside us, gazing up at Gwendolyn, holding a pad and pen.

In a sweet, teacher-sounding voice, she asked him, "Do you want my autograph?"

The boy nodded.

In tall bouncy letters she wrote: *With Love and Twirls, XO, Gwendolyn Parish.*

The boy smiled at the paper. His face went red as he backed away.

Gwendolyn looked suddenly sad. "I used to be like that," she said quietly.

I looked from the boy to her, trying to imagine what the two of them could have in common. "Like what?" I asked.

"Shy," she muttered under her breath, like it was a shameful disease.

"Really?" I said. "You sure don't seem shy."

She brushed a loose curl back. "I am," she whispered. "I have stage fright."

"But I just saw you onstage. You were great."

"My mother's taught me ways to compensate," she said, studying her nails. They were painted to match her lipstick. She changed the subject. "Are you here with anyone?"

"My grandma. How about you?"

She nodded toward the stage. Her mother hung on Jay

Valentine's arm, yakking away, beaming a hundred-watt smile.

"Do you want to go on a ride?" I asked. "I don't think my grandma'd mind."

"I'll see if it's all right," Gwendolyn said. When I started to follow her, she held her hand out. "Wait here."

Gwendolyn rushed toward the stage. As she spoke to her mother, she pointed toward where I stood waiting. Gwendolyn's mother stared at me—a deep, unbroken stare. A chill rippled through me. I hopped in place, rubbing the goose bumps away.

Gwendolyn returned, wearing a hangdog expression. "Sorry," she said. "My mother says it's been a long day. She thinks I need to rest."

I tried to hide my disappointment. I shrugged and said, "Some other time."

We stood there for a long moment—Gwendolyn fiddling with a poncho tassel, me rolling a pebble back and forth with my toe. It was like we both wanted to say something but couldn't think of what that something might be. "Well," I said, "I better find Gram."

Gwendolyn checked her watch. "I should go, too." She waved then turned, dragging her feet toward the stage. I watched her, thinking, For someone who's a big-time winner, that girl could look a whole lot happier.

Madame Paulina

Since I've been old enough to hold a dust cloth I've helped Gram with the Saturday morning cleaning chores. As I polished my bureau, I felt for the bag containing my Beatles 45. I'd slid it underneath my dresser scarf, hoping I'd get the nerve to ask Gram to play it on her phonograph. And that's when I remembered the number from the HELP WANTED sign I'd jotted down on my receipt. I fished it out of the bag, headed for the living room, and told Gram, "I've got a phone number for you."

She looked up from the knickknacks she was dusting. "Whose?"

"The Cut-n-Curl beauty parlor. They're looking for part-time help. I thought you might be interested." I set the small paper on the coffee table.

Gram didn't comment. Instead, she asked, "You done cleaning your room?"

I nodded.

"Did you remember to dust under your bed?"

"Yes, ma'am."

"And straighten inside your closet?"

"Uh-huh."

Gram tipped her head toward the kitchen. "See them dollar bills on the counter?"

Indeed, I did. There were two crisp ones. Except she'd already given me my allowance. "You got three days of vacation left before school starts," Gram said.

I wondered what she was getting at. "That's right," I agreed.

"I bet you'd love to waste one of them days hanging out at the county fair."

My heart raced, just thinking about it. "Well, sure, I would."

"And I reckon you'd enjoy wasting my money on that silly fair if you could."

"I reckon so, Gram. But, um, are you saying . . . ?"

She pointed her feather duster at me. "Be home by two o'clock sharp. Sears and Roebuck is running a sale on back-to-school dresses, and I plan to take you shopping."

"Thanks!" I yelled, grabbing the money and taking off— fast, before Gram had a chance to change her mind.

I hurried through the gate toward the funhouse, which was always my favorite attraction. I loved the rotating tunnel. I'd watch everybody slip and fall and clunk heads before crawling to the other side. Then I'd commence to strut straight through, leaving the whole lot of them gawking. See, I'd discovered the secret of the tunnel: You've got to walk *into* the wall curving toward you. Once you know that, it's a cinch.

Circling the midway, I prayed I'd spot Gwendolyn. I ate a chili cheese dog, drank a root beer float, and rode the carousel twice. I still had two quarters left. Normally I'd be itching to spend them. But even a county fair ain't much fun without somebody to share it with you. So I started toward the gate.

A woman in a long flowing dress stepped in front of me. Her long fingernails curled under like bird claws and her breath smelled like licorice whips. "Care to have your fortune told by Madame Paulina?" she asked me.

Gram would have a fit if she found out I'd spent money on a fortune-teller. She claimed hocus-pocus was the devil's work. Still, I was awful curious. "How much?"

"Twenty-five cents." She motioned toward a card table draped with a blue velvet cloth. A crystal ball sat in the center.

I dug a quarter out of my pocket, dropped it on the table, and sat down.

Madame Paulina sat across from me. She closed her eyes, moving her hands over the glass globe. "You have burning question?" she asked me.

"Plenty of 'em." I wiggled in my chair, getting comfortable. "My grandma says I've got more questions than Planter's has peanuts. How many do you want?"

She opened one eye. "One question per quarter, please."

I drummed the table, deciding what I wanted to know most. Except it was hard to concentrate. I kept getting sidetracked, thinking of the back-to-school shopping that awaited me. And that made me think of Bailey, and how I'd have to face my first day of school without her. "Am I ever gonna have another friend?" I blurted.

Madame Paulina's hands danced back and forth above the clear ball. She was quiet for so long I guessed she was trying to find a way to break the bad news to me. But when she spoke, she said, "You will have several friends."

"Several?" I repeated. "Are you sure?" Bailey had been my one and only friend since second grade. I was pretty rusty in the Meeting New People department.

"I see one friend in particular." She touched the glass. "A girl. She spends a great deal of time crying."

Surely Madame Paulina had me mixed up with somebody else. Like I said before, I ain't a crybaby. And I don't hang around with crybabies, either.

Her fake eyelashes fluttered. "I see a boy, too." She paused. "He likes you."

I made a face. "Do you mean *likes me* likes me?"

Madame Paulina nodded.

I stood, pushing my chair in. If that was the best fortune she could dream up—that I would meet a crybaby girl and a boy with a case of puppy love—I'd heard enough.

As I started to walk away, she called, "Wait! I see something else." She touched the crystal ball, tracing her finger in a small circle.

I turned, squinting down at the globe. I couldn't see a dadblasted thing.

"Do you want to know what it is?" she asked me.

"Do I have to pay another quarter to find out?"

"It's a penny," she told me.

I folded my arms. "Then how come I paid twenty-five cents last time?"

Madame Paulina smiled. "No. That is what I see in the crystal ball—a penny. One of those unusual pennies with the funny leaves on the back."

A shiver quivered up my spine. "Are you talking about a wheat penny?"

"Yes, a wheat penny." She tapped the glass globe. "There it is, in your future."

Ready, Set, Go

Sears and Roebuck had always been Gramps's favorite store. I loved following him down the escalator to the hardware department, peeking into the row of bins, learning the names of things: switch plates, breaker boxes, Allen wrenches, roofing nails. That's what I was thinking as Gram removed several size-ten girls' dresses from the sale rack, draping them across one arm. She nudged me toward a fitting room. "Need help?" she asked, hanging the dresses inside.

"I'll be fine," I said, closing the curtain. I slipped out of my T-shirt and shorts and yanked the first dress over my head. It was blue and green plaid with huge white buttons and a prickly lace collar that set me itching from the get-go. My bruised knees poked beneath the hem, shiny as a pair of Gram's prune plums. I didn't bother to tie the belt or fix my falling-down socks. I just pulled the divider aside so Gram could see for herself how ridiculous that dress looked.

Gram pinched the fabric on either side of my waist. "Fits you perfect," she said.

I held my tongue and glanced at the second dress, which was crawling with bright red polka dots. *At least they ain't pink*, I told myself, yanking the curtain closed.

School started on a Tuesday, the day after Labor Day.

I was eating breakfast when Gram paused beside me, wearing her favorite brown dress and matching pumps. My grandma, Eunice B. Colchester, has a set time for everything. A time for waking up and a time for going to bed. A time for starting supper and a time for sitting down to eat it. And in Gram's book, seven thirty in the morning is *not* Parading Around Dressed Like You're Heading Someplace Fancy time. It's Soaking in the Tub time.

"Why aren't you taking your bath?" I asked her.

"I took a shower instead."

Something was mighty fishy. "How come you're all gussied up?"

"'Cause I'm going with you to register. I want to make a good impression."

"Yeah?" I stood and put my bowl in the sink. "Whatcha got planned after that?"

Gram grabbed her pocketbook and handed me my lunch bag. "Nobody's shown an interest in buying that car yet, *or* the Beaver Creek house, and I got bills to pay." She reached inside her change purse, handing me three cents for milk money. "I figured I'd check out that hairdressing job you told me about."

Gram pulled the door closed, and we started up the dirt road, the morning sun at our backs. An inchworm fell out of nowhere, landing on my knuckle. I knew just how he felt, suddenly dropped someplace strange. I moved carefully, trying not to disturb him.

"Nice day," Gram said. "I sure don't miss that humidity." Gram had a whole kit and caboodle of things she didn't miss about Florida. Her list could stretch a city block—she'd never convince me Ohio was better than Florida.

Gram smoothed my bangs back. They were just shy of being long enough to tuck behind my ears. "If I get that job," she said, "maybe you'd like me to give you a permanent wave."

I hate it when grown-ups do that—try passing off a lamebrained idea as something *you* might want, when it's really their own personal hankering. I squinted down at the inchworm. He was making his way toward my wrist. "Thanks," I said. "But I like my hair the way it is."

Gram harrumphed. "Suit yourself."

We walked the rest of the way in silence.

Finally we reached the school. The wide front lawn was flooded with unfamiliar faces. I felt like a wrecker ball had walloped my middle. I held my stomach, thinking, You will never see Bailey Parncutt walking the halls of this school. Or Mr. Barnett, the custodian with the knock-knock jokes. Or Teddy and Freddy, the Dibble twins.

A man in a bright orange vest motioned us across the street.

Gram nudged me with her elbow. "Ready, Itch?"

Of course I wasn't ready. Still, I started walking. When we got to the other side, I told Gram, "I'd like you to call me Delores from now on."

"Oh?" She raised one eyebrow. "Why's that?"

I kicked a pebble. "It's just a feeling I've got."

Two girls ran past, their dresses billowing behind them. They were both wearing kneesocks and penny loafers. I glanced at my ankle socks and Keds, sighing deeply.

Gram held the door open for me. I paused, staring down the long hallway. The floor was so waxy it looked wet. The air smelled of wintergreen paste.

I remembered the inchworm and decided to check on his progress.

Lucky bum, he was up and gone.

First Day

Gramps once told me that if you really wanted something, you had to want it with every freckle, eyelash, and toenail. Everywhere I went—the library, the lavatory, the cafeteria—I kept an eye out for Gwendolyn. I even practiced how I'd respond when I saw her. First, I'd open my mouth, looking surprised. I would do this casually, so as not to look desperate for a friend. Then I'd say, "Hey, I know you," narrowing my eyes, like I was straining to recall her name. "Gwendolyn, right?"

But there was no sign of her.

During lunch, I ate alone. At recess, I parked myself beneath a tree. I was about to begin reading the book I'd checked out of the school library that morning when I felt somebody watching me. I glanced up.

A boy stepped beneath the roof of leaves. "I *thought* that was you. I saw you the other day at Lazy Acres. You were sleeping in a car," he said.

"And you're the paperboy," I replied, happy to be recognized.

"That's me." He paused, like he was thinking what to say next. "So, how long've you lived in Lakeville?"

"Almost two weeks." Actually, it was twelve days, sixteen

hours, and—I checked my watch—forty minutes. But what the heck.

"You like it so far?" he asked.

I shrugged. "I like Florida better."

"Wow. I didn't know you're from Florida. I've been wanting to go there ever since I seen this TV show about the Everglades. You guys got live alligators down there."

"Yeah, we do. Lots of them." I didn't bother to inform him I'd never seen one.

When he jammed his hands in his pockets, I noticed his trousers were huge. A ratty belt was pulled tight, holding those britches in place. The cuffs had been rolled several times. I thought of Bailey and the too-big dresses her mama'd loan her for school.

The paperboy held out a pack of Black Jack. "Here," he said. "You wanna piece?"

Gum wasn't allowed on school grounds, but if he was willing to risk getting caught, so was I. "Sure," I said, reaching for a stick and unwrapping it.

Across the playground kids shrieked and screamed. But underneath that tree all was quiet—except for the sound of Black Jack getting the daylights chewed out of it.

"I'm Billy, by the way. What's your name?"

"Delores," I answered.

"Really? I got an Aunt Delores. She's a grouchy old biddy. Oh, but"—he blushed—"that don't mean I'm saying you are. 'Cause you seem nice enough."

"Thanks," I said, fighting a smile.

The lunch monitor blew her whistle, lining everybody up.

"Well." Billy gulped hard. "See you around, maybe?"

I'd only swallowed chewing gum once. I made the mistake of doing it in front of Gram, who gave me a royal what-for, saying how my stomach would take seven long years to digest it. I gulped, too. "Yeah," I said. "See you around."

Gram and Cousin Effie were sitting outside clipping recipes when I got home.

I waved and walked on past.

Gram looked up. "What's the hurry? How'd your first day of school go?"

I didn't feel like admitting that the one and only high point was shooting the breeze with our paperboy. "So-so."

"Make any new friends?" she asked.

"I'm working on it." I started toward the trailer again.

Now it was Cousin Effie's turn to stop me. "What's your teacher's name?"

I sighed, faced her, and answered, "Mrs. Meriwether."

"Bet she's all sunny days and blue skies," she said, poking Gram's arm, guffawing. "Get it, Eunice? *Merry* weather?"

Cousin Effie was nice enough, but she wasn't the brightest crayon in the box. "Excuse me," I said, forcing a smile. "I'm gonna start my homework."

When I reached the steps, Gram cleared her throat loudly.

"Oh, yeah." I turned once more. "How'd everything go at the Cut-n-Curl?"

Gram sat straight up in her seat. "Trudy and I got on swimmingly. I start tomorrow morning."

"Congratulations," I said, hurrying up the steps. That time they both let me go.

An envelope with Bailey's handwriting was propped against the sugar bowl. *Thank goodness,* I thought, tearing the flap. Surely, Bailey's letter would cheer me up.

There were two drawings inside. I unfolded them, flattening the creases. The first was of the Beaver Creek Bowling Alley, where Bailey's older brother Curtis worked setting up pins. Bailey and I used to visit him on our days off school. If business was slow, he'd let us bowl a free game. The second was a sketch of a kitten. I scratched my head, wondering why Bailey thought I'd be interested. She knew I wasn't fond of cats and how they pranced around like spoiled brats, scratching whoever they pleased.

I opened Bailey's letter, praying Becky Montgomery's family had moved back to Atlanta and taken their lipstick samples with them. *Dear Delores,* Bailey wrote.

I miss you! I miss you! I miss you!
And Annabelle misses you, too. I visited her at the swamp yesterday, but I was so bored without you there, I only stayed five minutes.
Mama's letting me wear my lipstick to school. Teddy Dibble says it makes me look older. I'm

saving my money so I can buy nail polish to match.

For Show and Tell last Friday Becky Montgomery brought in a picture of her cat Cleopatra and her seven kittens. When they're old enough to be separated, Becky's going to give them away. I'm sending you a picture of the one I want. He's gray with white feet, and Becky calls him Snoopy 'cause he's nosy and gets into everything.

I folded Bailey's letter closed. "Snoopy's a *dog* name," I grumbled.

Collision Course

Wednesday, there was still no sign of Gwendolyn. On Thursday my luck changed.

I moseyed past the crossing guard. Just ahead, a white Ford Fairlane veered to the curb. I'd learned to recognize automobiles from Gramps. He used to quiz me when we went for a drive. "Quick," he'd say, picking a car that was speeding by so fast I couldn't cheat and read the name, "what's that one called?" And I'd shout, "Chevy Impala!" or "Cadillac Eldorado!" or "Buick Electra!" After he was done testing me, Gramps would pat my shoulder and say, "You done good, Itch." Never "You done good *for a girl*." I appreciated that about him.

The passenger door on the Fairlane opened. A girl in a red dress stepped out clutching a lunchbox, waving at the man inside. He waved back, tooted, and drove off.

"Gwendolyn!" I called, forgetting everything I'd practiced in my How Not to Look Desperate for a Friend plan.

Gwendolyn turned, smiling. "I remember you from the county fair. Diane, right?"

"Delores," I said, smiling back.

"Delores. Sorry." Gwendolyn started toward the playground, her Lassie lunchbox swinging at her side. I fell into step beside her, clutching my paper sack. Gwendolyn leaned into my shoulder, like she was about to tell me a secret. Quietly, she said, "At school I go by Wendy. I only use Gwendolyn for performance purposes."

'Sakes alive. She sounded like she should be having tea with the queen of England. "Wendy," I repeated, then added, "I kept thinking I'd run into you—"

"I was absent." She coughed a fake-sounding cough. "Summer cold."

We passed a circle of little kids playing Duck Duck Goose. "Who's your teacher gonna be?" I asked, hoping she would say Mrs. Meriwether. There were two empty desks in my room, and one was right next to mine.

Wendy glanced around, like she was searching for someone. "Mrs. Lovejoy."

"Oh," I moaned, without meaning to.

She turned quickly. "What did you hear about her?"

I couldn't rightly fess up to *why* I'd moaned. After all, what if Wendy didn't feel like being in the same class as me? I decided on a little white lie. "I, um, heard she gives a lot of homework is all."

"Great. Like I've got time for extra assignments."

"What do you mean?"

She brushed a curl back. "I'm really busy."

"Busy with what?"

"Dance lessons. In Cleveland."

"Wow. That's kind of far away, isn't it?"

She nodded. "Forty-five minutes each way. There's a studio in Pepper Pike that's closer, but my mother insists I study with Minerva Stern. She's the best in the state. Anyway"—Wendy lifted her chin, scanning the crowd again—"I have to do my homework in the car, which isn't fun because I get motion sickness. Once, I actually threw up."

I shook my head, sympathizing. And not just 'cause I wanted Wendy to be my friend. I felt bad for her. I'd only thrown up twice in my life, and I prayed there'd never be a third time. "What night's your lesson?" I asked.

"Tuesday is ballet. Wednesday is twirling. Advanced twirling is Thursday, and Friday is modern dance. That makes four recitals to prepare for. Plus I have two solos."

I couldn't imagine being that busy. "How about Mondays?"

"The studio's closed. Plus, Monday is the day my mother gets her hair done."

Across the playground, two girls wheeled their matching

Schwinns toward the bike rack. When Wendy noticed them, her face lit up. "Just who I was looking for!" she cried, excited. I was so jealous I could spit. *I* wanted to make someone's face light up like that. She tugged my sleeve and said, "Come with me. Meet Anna Marie and Connie."

I followed her, but we didn't get far.

A redheaded boy raced toward us, weaving willy-nilly. A kid with a crew cut chased after him, shaking his fist, yelling, "You're in big trouble, Applegate!"

"Watch out!" I called to Wendy, trying to steer her out of their path. Except I wasn't fast enough. The redheaded boy barreled smack-dab into her. Wendy's lunchbox soared across the blue sky, slamming the flagpole, letting out a huge metal clang.

The kid with the crew cut veered off. The redheaded boy collapsed against a tree. When he looked up, I called "Billy!" at the exact same moment he called "Delores!" in return.

Apologies and Promises

Wendy knelt on the grass, flipping her lunchbox open. She shook her thermos, and the glass clinked around inside. "You're a clumsy oaf, Billy Applegate!"

Billy doubled forward, a hand on each knee, attempting

to catch his breath. "I—I'm sorry," he panted. "Look, I—I got a paper route. I'll buy you a brand-new one."

Judging from the size of the holes in his sneakers, I'd guess Billy hadn't seen the sunny side of brand-new in some time. I sat beside Wendy on the damp grass. The back of my dress would soon be soaked, but I didn't let that stop me. When you're trying to make friends with somebody, you can't let a wet behind get in the way.

Billy stood, pinching a cramp in his side. "Whaddaya think?"

Wendy slipped the busted thermos in its holder and slammed the lunchbox closed. Obviously, she wasn't feeling forgiving.

I felt bad for Billy, standing there looking dumb as mud, waiting for Wendy's answer. "It's okay," I told him. "Wendy knows it was an accident. Right, Wendy?"

Wendy didn't answer. She scowled as a school bus pulled to the curb, burping black smoke. Honestly, I couldn't see somebody getting so upset about a dumb thermos.

"Well, sorry again," Billy said, hurrying off.

I had witnessed dozens of Bailey's hissy fits, and I knew just what to do: Sit on the sidelines till they passed. But I had no idea what worked with Gwendolyn Parish. As I tried to decide what to say, I recalled something Gramps told me the day I lost my favorite harmonica in the swamp. *Objects are replaceable, Itch. People ain't. Best save your tears for them.*

I breathed a slow, sad sigh, a Missing Gramps sigh I

could feel clear down to my toes. "Wendy," I said softly, "it's only a thermos. People matter way more than things."

The bus door opened. Kids poured out, clamoring behind us.

Wendy moped toward the door, mumbling, "Try telling that to my mother."

While Mrs. Meriwether read to us from *The Witch of Blackbird Pond*, I was hunkered down in my seat, thinking of one single thing: how to replace Wendy's Lassie thermos. *Come on*, I told my brain. *Surely you can come up with something. You'll be one step closer to having yourself a new friend if you do.*

My pep talk worked. By dismissal, I was reeling in a winner.

I waited by the front door for Wendy. The weather had warmed up since recess, and the sun felt nice on my back. When Wendy appeared, I said hi, smiling widely.

"Hi," she said back. I'd added *insipid* to my Favorite Words list in fifth grade. It means weak or namby-pamby. And the smile Wendy offered me was insipid.

I glanced at the spot where her father'd dropped her off that morning. "Is your dad picking you up?" I asked.

"No." Wendy squinted into the sun. "He only gives me a ride in the morning, on his way to the office. He usually works late. After school I walk."

So far so good. "Do you, um"—I hesitated—"walk home with anybody?"

"I used to, before Anna Marie and Connie bought *twin Schwinns*." She rolled her eyes.

I nodded, fighting a grin. "Which way are you headed?"

She gestured toward the wide, tree-lined street leading to downtown Lakeville. "Two blocks past the center of town," she answered, "in the historic district."

"I'm heading that way, too," I said, leaving off the part about living *nine* blocks past the center of town, in a mobile home park. "Mind if I join you?"

Wendy shrugged her shoulders. "Sure. Why not?"

When we reached the fairgrounds, Wendy stopped. Setting her lunchbox and books on the ground, she leaned into the metal fence, weaving her fingers through the links. I stopped beside her and did the same.

The rides were gone, and the livestock building was boarded up. The ground was littered with flattened snow cone cups. The outdoor stage seemed tiny. Tiny and lonely and forgotten.

"I shouldn't have won the talent show," Wendy mumbled.

My jaw dropped. "But you deserved to win. You were the best performer there."

Wendy shook her head. "I made three major mistakes."

"Well," I said, "they must have been invisible, because I couldn't see—"

"My mother saw them," Wendy interrupted. "She knows my routines by heart. Some she even helps choreograph."

She squeezed the chain links so hard her knuckles went white. "I'm just naturally clumsy. My mother thought ballet would correct the problem, but I still stub my toes and bump into walls and break things."

"Heck, everybody does that."

"I'm not supposed to be like *everybody*," she said.

Silence hung between us, thick as tree sap.

I glanced down at Wendy's lunchbox. "Is that why you're worried about the thermos? Because your mother'll think you broke it?"

Wendy looked away. "Something like that."

The time felt right to tell her what I'd come up with. "Where'd your mother buy your Lassie lunchbox set?"

"Woolworth's. Why?"

"Because I have an idea for getting you a new thermos."

Wendy turned to face me. "I'm listening."

"My grandma has this new job at the Cut-n-Curl. We can stop there right now. I'll ask for an advance on my allowance. If Gram says yes, we'll go to Woolworth's and buy a new set. I'll keep the lunchbox and we can swap thermoses."

Her forehead creased as she thought. "But then *you* won't have a thermos."

"I don't need one," I said. "I buy milk."

Wendy's eyes narrowed. "Why are you offering to do this?"

"Just to help is all."

Wendy thought some more. Finally, she said, "All right. On one condition. You can't tell anyone. Promise?"

I remembered the last promise I'd made—that I would help Bailey babysit once the twins were born—a promise I was forced to break. It was nice to have a shot at a new one. I pretend-zipped my lip and drew a giant X across my chest.

Wendy stooped to pick up her stuff. "Let's try out that idea of yours."

Thank You, Mrs. Ferris

Just inside the Cut-n-Curl was a wall filled with framed photographs. Some were scenes of downtown Lakeville, but most were pictures of people—a waitress serving pie at the diner, two girls jumping rope behind the school, a boy waving a Cleveland Indians pennant. I studied a photo of a small blond girl with a short pixie haircut. Her toes pointed in and she fiddled with the hem on her skirt. A woman, dressed fancy as a fashion model, stood next to her.

"Hey, Wendy," I said, "isn't that you and your mom?"

She nodded. "We were at a library fund-raiser. I was only four." She squinted at the picture. "Look at the way I'm standing. I hadn't learned a *thing* about stage presence."

"Stage presence?"

"You know, how to present myself. Like *she's* doing." Wendy tapped her mother's face, and I noticed how short her nails were. Short and rough, like she'd bitten them down to the quick.

Wendy cleared her throat, reminding me of why we were there. "Don't forget," she whispered, "the lunchbox and thermos set is for you."

"I remember," I whispered back, and we started toward Gram's styling station.

Gram was setting a lady's hair in rollers. The lady was round as a navel orange, and her hair was the color of one, too. When Gram was finished, she motioned toward the dryers. She wound a timer, lowering a dome over Orange Lady's head. Several moments later, she looked up. "What in Sam Hill are you doing here?" she said, walking toward us. She was wearing an apron I hadn't seen on her since she had her own beauty parlor. When she stopped beside me, I could smell our old house in the fabric.

I was jittery as all get-out. "Will Trudy mind that I stopped by?" I asked her.

"Trudy left to go shopping," Gram answered. "It's Triple Green Stamps Day at the plaza." She tipped her chin toward Wendy. "Ain't you forgetting your manners?"

"Sorry. This is Gwendolyn Parish. Wendy, this is my grandma, Mrs. Colchester."

Gram studied Wendy's face. "Why, you're the girl who won the talent show."

Wendy nodded. "Yes, ma'am."

"That's some gift the good Lord blessed you with," Gram told her.

I considered informing Gram that the good Lord was only partly responsible for Wendy's talent. Her nightly trips to Cleveland had lots to do with it, too. But I stayed quiet. It's wise not to step between Gram and the Lord.

"So," Gram said, "what brings you two here?"

"Well," I started. Then I stalled. Wendy nudged me with her elbow. "I, um, have a, well, a . . . favor to ask you."

Gramps once said there are two things you'd have to fight to get away from Gram: money and the last ear of corn. Gram's face soured. "What kind of favor?"

When I opened my mouth to speak, Orange Lady's timer dinged. As Gram walked to the corner, lifting the dryer dome, I motioned toward the small waiting area. "Over there," I whispered to Wendy. "I'll meet you as soon as I'm done."

Gram undid a roller, felt the hair that clung to it, then patted Orange Lady's shoulder. "You're dry. I'll be back in two shakes, Mrs. Ferris."

My, I thought, *what a perfect name for somebody big and round as a Ferris wheel.*

Gram returned, looking a tad grouchy. "You were fixing to ask me for a favor?"

Mrs. Ferris glanced in our direction. She flipped a magazine page, like she intended to read it, pretending to mind her own business. Avoiding Gram's eyes, I said, "I noticed the girls in my class use lunchboxes instead of paper bags."

Gram whipped a rat-tail comb out of the disinfectant. "That so?"

I shook my head yes. "I was thinking, maybe . . . maybe . . . maybe . . ." I sounded like a record with a skip in it.

"Let me guess." Gram pointed the comb at me. "If you had a lunchbox, you'd feel more like the other girls."

I nodded, relieved.

Gram walked away. "You know I don't question how you spend your allowance."

"But, Gram"—I followed her, motioning for Wendy to stay put. "I don't get my allowance till Saturday."

Gram led Mrs. Ferris toward the styling station. "Mmm-hmmm."

I glanced at Wendy, who was staring out Trudy's front window. I knew anything could happen between that moment and Saturday. Why, Anna Marie or Connie might bike past and just *give* Wendy their thermos. They probably had plenty of extras.

Mrs. Ferris dropped into her seat, smiling up at me. I smiled back, to be polite.

"Gram—" I started.

"I'll see you at home," she interrupted. Gram didn't appreciate me not taking no for an answer.

But I couldn't let Wendy down. Even if Gram pitched a fit, I had to try again. I stepped closer, watching her in the mirror. "Gram," I said, "please, let me finish. I was hoping I could get that lunchbox set today. I mean, it's really hard fitting in at a new school. People are all the time noticing ways you're different from them. . . ." My hands were sweating. I patted them dry on my dress. That's when I realized— I wasn't telling an all-out fib. Sure, I was aiming to replace Wendy's busted thermos. But maybe I was looking to fix something broken inside of me, too. *I* needed that lunch-box set.

"Pardon me for butting in," Mrs. Ferris piped up, "but I have five grandchildren of my own. And, like I always tell my daughter, Mary Ellen, 'Face it, sweetie, even when Mama says no, Grandma's gonna say yes'."

Gram scowled. "What are you saying, Mrs. Ferris?"

Mrs. Ferris nodded my way. "Your granddaughter's mama must've said no. . . ."

A sudden, dull ache filled my chest. Mrs. Ferris had no idea how many things my mama'd said no to. Like sticking around and attempting to be a mama, for starters. When I turned to face Gram I caught my reflection in the glass. The person staring back at me was a stranger, some droopy-faced girl I'd never seen before.

Gram's eyes met mine in the mirror. Her scowl faded, and the lines that etched her forehead grew soft.

Maybe that strange girl's face took her by surprise, too. Or maybe Gram decided she wasn't looking to make any enemies her second day on the job. I'm not sure which. But I could've hugged Mrs. Ferris silly when Gram tipped her head toward the back room, mumbling, "Go on, fetch me my pocketbook."

Fog

I motioned toward the bench outside Woolworth's. Wendy sat beside me and we opened our matching lunchboxes. Mine had a new-store scent, and Wendy's smelled like baloney and mustard.

"Here," I said, holding out my thermos.

Wendy just stared at it.

"What's wrong?" I asked her.

"I still don't understand how you're going to explain *this*"—Wendy shook her broken thermos—"when your grandmother gave you money for something brand-new."

I took the busted container from her and unscrewed the lid. I stood, dumping the glass bits and juice in a trash can. "I told you. I buy milk, so I don't need one." I screwed the lid back on. "I'll put your thermos in the back of our pantry. Gram'll never notice."

"What about your mother? Maybe she will."

Between having a southern accent and living in a mobile home park, I already felt different enough without dragging my mama into the picture. "I don't live with her," I said. "Only my grandma. I used to live with my grandpa, too. But, well, he died."

"Oh. Sorry." Wendy took the new thermos, placing it inside her box. She glanced down at the Almond Joy I'd bought with the change I had left.

I peeled the wrapper back. I took one half and handed Wendy the other.

"Thanks," she said, biting into it.

We sat there, our matching lunchboxes propped on our knees, chewing away.

A hawk flew across the sky. I stared up at him, waiting for the moment I loved most—when he stopped flapping his wings and glided, making time stand still.

"Wendy," I said softly, "why were you so worried? What would've happened if you'd come home with a busted thermos?"

Wendy hesitated so long I thought she'd decided not to answer. "That would depend on my mother's mood," she said, finally. "If she's had a good day, she might not have much to say."

"And if she's had a bad day . . . ?"

Wendy rested her hands on her lunchbox, drumming the top with her fingers. "There could be trouble."

"What kind of trouble?"

Wendy stood, collecting her books. "I have to go or I'll be late for my dance lesson."

I touched her arm lightly. "What kind of trouble?"

"Just . . . trouble."

Wendy walked away. Her words hung between us, like

the ribbons of fog that snaked across the swamp back in Beaver Creek.

No way, nohow, could you see past that fog.

You had to wait till it lifted.

Part Two

The Scoop

As I walked past Cousin Effie's door, she hollered, "Eunice just phoned. She wanted me to tell you she'll be home around five. Want some strawberry-rhubarb pie while you're waiting?"

I spared Effie the details—that (1) rhubarb gives me the trots, and (2) I was well past the age where I needed babysitting. "No, thank you," I called back.

Gram had left me a snack on the table, but I was too tired to chew. I opened my lunchbox and dragged a stepstool to the pantry, tucking Wendy's thermos in a far corner.

My homework was waiting for me, but I needed to rest my brain. I headed outside to the Bel Air, trying hard to ignore the FOR SALE sign Gram had returned to the windshield. I slipped into the backseat and rolled down the windows, taking several long, slow breaths. I pictured Gramps sitting up front, smiling as Frank Sinatra crooned on the radio. "Gramps," I said, right out loud. My heart was filled with missing him, and I needed to hear his name. "Gramps," I said, again, touching his seat. The FOR SALE sign glared at me, and my eyes filled.

A sudden sound startled me. I bolted upright, smacking my noggin on the ceiling. I half expected to see Gram's face poke through the window, asking me why I was dillydally-ing when my assignments weren't done.

Instead, Billy Applegate appeared, his bike tires snap-ping gravel as he flung a newspaper at our door. It whapped against the screen, then dropped to the stoop below.

I sat extra still, praying he wouldn't see me. If there's one thing worse than being a crybaby, it's being a crybaby caught in the act.

Billy paused. He cleared his throat. "Delores? Is that you?"

I wiped my nose. "I'm kind of in the middle of some-thing."

He wheeled closer. Some people can't take a hint. "I was just wondering if you could tell Wendy Parish something for me. I counted my savings, and I'm pretty sure I got enough to buy her a new thermos." He reached in his pocket, jingling change.

It's probably all pennies, I thought. But when I glanced at his holey-toed sneakers again, I softened. "Don't worry, I bou—" I stopped myself, remembering my promise. "Wendy already got herself a new one."

"Are you and Wendy Parish *friends*?" Billy smirked.

"Maybe," I half said, half snapped. "Who wants to know?"

Billy looked flustered. "Aw, nerts, I didn't mean nothin' bad. It's just that you're nice, and Wendy's friends are all hoity-toity. The kids call 'em the Breck Girls."

"How come?" I asked.

"Ain't you noticed?" He rested a hand on his hip, girly-style. "They look like the models in the Breck Shampoo commercial." He pursed his lips and fluffed his hair.

I smiled. "You do that good. Better than I could."

"Thanks . . . I think." Billy pressed his bangs flat. "I'm glad everything worked out okay with Wendy's thermos. I wouldn't want her gettin' into hot water 'cause of me."

"Whaddaya mean?" I asked.

Billy scratched his ear. "You haven't heard the scoop on Wendy's mama?"

"No." I leaned my arm on the window frame. "Tell me."

"She isn't the nicest lady in Lakeville. Ever see the movie *Dr. Jekyll and Mr. Hyde?*"

"Yeah. I watched it on TV with my grandpa. Why?"

"That's how Mrs. Parish is, full of surprises." He paused, straightening his tire toward the road. "Well, I better get going. If Mrs. Templeton's newspaper ain't on the step when her husband gets home from work, I'm out a tip this month."

I cleared the supper table while Gram packed my lunch. She'd given me the same thing every day since I started carrying one in first grade: a sandwich, potato chips, an apple, and dessert. On Monday, the sandwich was peanut butter and jelly; on Tuesday, baloney and cheese. Wednesday meant egg salad; Thursday, canned SPAM; and on Friday she made tuna fish.

While Gram mixed the StarKist with mayonnaise, I stacked the dishes in the sink. When I heard her unsnap the latches on my new lunchbox, I froze.

"Didn't this come with a thermos?" she asked me.

"I, um—I already put it in the pantry." My throat felt dry. I started coughing.

Gram patted my back. "You all right?"

I looked away. "I'm fine. Why?"

Gram held up a slice of Wonder bread. "You turned white as this a second ago. Are you comin' down with something?" She lifted her hand to feel my forehead.

"No, ma'am," I said, ducking her touch, turning on the tap water full blast.

Lunch with the Breek Girls

"Delores!" Wendy called. "Wait up!"

My toes squirmed inside my Keds. I turned, smiling at our matching lunchboxes.

Wendy stopped beside me in the milk line. "Are you buying milk?" I asked her.

"No, I have apple juice." She shook her lunchbox. The thermos jostled against the metal sides. I loved the sound it made—*kalunka-lunka-lunk*. She leaned closer. "I just wanted to thank you again for the thermos. Last night was crazy at my house. My mother's car ran out of gas on the way to my lesson. We had to walk to the Shell station, and I missed the entire class. My mother was furious at my father for not checking the gauge before we left. Anyway"—Wendy gave her lunchbox another shake—"I was happy not to have to add *this* to the chaos."

"I'm glad I could help," I told her.

Wendy glanced across the cafeteria at Anna Marie and Connie, who sat peeling back the wax paper on their sandwiches. "Well." Wendy smiled. "Thank you again, Delores." When she turned to leave, my heart sank.

A girl wearing a dress that was way too big on her paused beside the milk line. She rummaged in her pocket, drawing out a small paper ticket. It looked like the card Bailey had to show the cafeteria ladies to prove she got free lunch. Suddenly, I would've yanked out my eyeteeth to have Bailey appear.

The lunch lady held out my milk, and I dropped my pennies in her palm.

I was so lost in my thoughts I completely missed Wendy's return. "Yoo hoo," she called, snapping her fingers in my face.

Shaking my head to clear the cobwebs, I said, "Sorry. What's up?"

"I've been thinking," Wendy said. "I'd like you to eat lunch at my table today."

I remembered what Billy had said. *Wendy's friends are all hoity-toity.*

Then Madame Paulina's face flashed before me. *I see several new friends.*

Wendy waited, watching me. "Well, what do you think?"

I gulped hard. "Sure," I said, "lead the way."

Wendy stopped at the end of her table. "Girls," she said, "this is Delores Colchester, the new girl from Florida. I've asked her to join us for lunch. Delores, this is Anna Marie Armstrong and Constance Talbot."

The lights shimmered on Anna Marie's black braids. Constance's red hair shone bright as Gram's copper teakettle. No wonder kids called them the Breck Girls.

"Pleased to meet you," I said.

Wendy hugged her skirt to her legs, swinging her foot over the long bench. I attempted to copy her, but my toe caught in my hem. I hopped on one foot, tugging till it yanked loose with a loud ripping noise.

Constance giggled. Anna Marie just stared.

"I never liked this dress anyway," I joked, trying to hide my embarrassment. I sat down, smiling a nervous smile. "I hope it's okay that Wendy asked me to sit here."

Anna Marie's face was so sour you'd think she'd swallowed a whole bag of lemon drops. "Of course it's okay," Constance said, nudging her. "Isn't it, Anna Marie?"

Anna Marie ripped the crust off her bread. "Yes. For today. Except usually"—she shot Wendy a look—"we discuss these things first."

Wendy shrugged. She unsnapped her lunchbox, inspecting what was inside.

Constance smiled at me. "Call me Connie," she said, sliding one of her Tootsie Rolls across the table, parking it beside my lunchbox. "It's not a trade. You can have it."

"Thanks," I said, opening my wrapper at the exact same second she opened hers. I chewed till the Tootsie Roll dissolved, then slid my tongue across my front teeth, making sure all the brown globs were gone.

I could feel Anna Marie studying me. "So," she said, "I hear your grandmother works at Trudy's Cut-n-Curl."

"Yeah. I mean, yes. She just started."

Connie sucked milk through her straw. "My mom gets her hair done at Trudy's."

"Mine, too," Wendy added.

Anna Marie rolled her eyes. "*Everyone's* mom gets her hair done at Trudy's."

Everyone's except mine, I thought.

Connie said, "Last week Trudy gave my mom a permanent wave. Trudy said it'll be easier for her to take care of during the holidays while she's working."

Anna Marie wrinkled her nose. "Your mother has a *job*?"

"Not a *job* job," Connie answered. "She's selling her artwork."

"Does she draw pictures?" I asked, hoping I'd get the chance to brag about Bailey.

Connie shook her head. "No, she crochets things to sell. She's got a craft fair coming up this weekend. We've had

SPAM casserole three nights in a row because she's busy trying to finish two hundred toilet paper holders."

Wendy snickered. "*Toilet* paper holders?"

Connie nodded. "The top part is a plastic doll body—a half a doll body, actually. My mom crochets the doll a skirt that fits over a spare roll of toilet paper."

Wendy leaned forward. "Did she make that up all by herself?"

"No," Connie answered. "She saw it in a magazine. Except my mom makes the skirts multicolored instead of single-colored like they showed in the picture. 'Artistic license,' she calls it."

When the bell rang for outdoor recess, none of us had finished eating. We stood, dumping our leftovers in the trash.

Connie nudged Wendy's side. "Weren't you wearing tights earlier?"

She was right. That morning I'd noticed Wendy's tan tights matched the stripes in her dress exactly. In fact, every time I'd seen Wendy she was wearing tights.

"I spilled juice on them during morning snack," Wendy answered, tugging her dress. "The nurse let me wash them in her office. I checked before lunch, but they weren't dry yet."

Out of nowhere, Wendy grabbed my arm. She called back to Anna Marie and Connie, "Meet us at the jump ropes. Delores and I call first up!" And her thermos *kalunka-lunka-lunk*ed at her side as we hurried through the door to the playground.

Shhhhh

The sky was concrete gray, and the air smelled like a pair of damp socks.

Wendy dug through the recess gear, tossing aside Frisbees and basketballs and catcher's mitts. Personally, I would've liked the mitt, but Wendy went straight for the jump rope.

Anna Marie and Connie took the wooden ends, twirling. Wendy skipped into the whirring arc, her blond curls jouncing. I hopped in afterwards, facing her. We held our skirts in place, jumping in unison.

I'd only jumped rope a few times. I wouldn't call it my favorite thing to do. I prefer activities where something might actually happen. Like if you go fishing, you *might* hook a fish. Or if you play ball, you *might* hit a homer or catch a fly. There's no guarantee, but there's a chance, at least. You can't say as much for jumping rope. All you do is bounce up and down, praying your lunch'll stay put.

The clouds grew thick, sinking lower. Wind whistled through the trees. Wendy sang, "Cinderella, dressed in yellow, went upstairs to kiss a fellow."

I'd heard that stupid chant so many times I'd memorized it without even trying. "By mistake she kissed a snake," I joined in. "How many doctors did it take?"

"One." *Jump.*

"Two." *Jump.*

"Three." *Jump.*

"Four." *Jump.*

Again the wind blew. The jump rope quivered.

"Five." *Jump.*

"Six." *Jump.*

"Seven." *Jump.*

"Eight—" A stronger gust whipped past, jerking the rope clean out of Connie's hand. Its wooden handle boomeranged, cracking me good in the ankle. But instead of grabbing my foot, like I normally would, I reached for the bottom of my dress, tugging it down around my knees.

Wendy wasn't quite as fast. Her skirt opened like a parachute and she shrieked, reaching for the flailing fabric.

The recess monitor blew her whistle. Anna Marie and Connie hurried away, dragging the jump rope behind them.

I stayed put, waiting for Wendy. And as she struggled to anchor her skirt in place, I saw them. Welts. Row after row, raised and red, lining the backs of Wendy's thighs.

I'd only seen marks like those once before. Back in Beaver Creek, two-faced Lenny Potts treated his son, Lenny Junior, like his own personal punching bag. I shared a cubby with Lenny Junior in first grade. One day, while he was taking off his rain slicker, his shirt rode up. Welts lined poor Lenny Junior's back. They ain't something you forget.

Slowly, Wendy lifted her head.

A raindrop plinked on my forehead. Another landed on my cheek. Soon there were too many to keep track of.

The monitor blew her whistle a second time. The stragglers ran past us, dodging the sudden deluge.

Wendy reached for our lunchboxes and handed me mine. Our eyes met. Tiny raindrops clung to the tips of her lashes.

"Wendy," I blurted out, before I lost my nerve, "I saw your legs, the welts, I—"

Thunder split the sky.

Wendy held a finger to her lips. "Shhhh," she said softly. Then she looped her arm through mine, leading us both toward the door. "Walk with me to the nurse's office," she said calmly. "My tights should be dry by now."

Endings

When the rain stopped, the air smelled fresh, like a set of just-washed sheets. I wished my brain could get cleaned out that same way, because everywhere I turned, I saw welts.

I opened the door to our mobile home, surprised to find Gram parked on the davenport, watching *The Edge of Night*.

Her snack—Ritz crackers and squirt cheese—sat on the end table beside her.

"Hi," I said. "How come you aren't working?"

"Business was slow," Gram mumbled. "Trudy sent me home early." Her eyes were glued to the TV. Gramps once joked that if President Johnson had to declare the world was coming to an end, he'd best time it during a commercial.

When the station break came on, Gram still didn't look up.

I walked over, sitting beside her. "Is something wrong?" I asked.

Gram shook the cheese can and squirted an orange blob on a cracker. Then she popped it in her mouth whole. "Vah houf," she said, chewing.

"Vah houf?" I repeated. "What's that mean?"

Gram swallowed. "*The house.* In Beaver Creek. I got a phone call today. Somebody's made an offer on it."

I collapsed backwards against the cushions. I knew Gram and I would never move back to that house. But I hadn't pictured anyone else living there, either.

"They'd like to be in by Christmas," she added.

I stood up fast. "But that's only three months away. What'd you say?"

Gram scowled at me. "There's a FOR SALE sign on the front lawn, Itch—excuse me, Delores. What do you suppose I said?"

I was fuming. I had to get mad at somebody, and Gram was the only person handy.

When her soap opera came back on, she said, "Delores, sit down or move, please. You're standing in the way of the television."

I didn't budge. "I miss that house," I said, raising my voice over Gram's program. "I hate living in this stupid trailer."

She eyed me sternly. "Delores, watch your tongue."

I'd never back-talked Gram. But suddenly, without knowing why or how, I'd stepped somewhere I'd never gone before. Maybe my nerves were raw from seeing Wendy's welts. Or maybe I was just plain sick and tired of doing everything Gram's way. "You're getting rid of all the things that proved Gramps existed," I half spoke, half hollered. "The house, his belongings"—I glared at her—"his *car*. You act like you're fixing to erase him!"

Gram sat there, stone silent.

"Aren't you gonna say something?" I demanded. "Aren't you gonna warn me never to talk that way again? Or send me to my room, or give me extra chores? Huh?"

Her face took on an odd, un-Gram expression. And as the lines in her forehead smoothed and a softness settled in her jaw and a tear inched down her cheek, I knew why she looked strange.

I'd never seen Gram cry.

Each day that next week, I ate lunch with the Breck Girls.

And each day Anna Marie studied me like a specimen underneath a microscope.

Wendy and I settled into an after-school routine. We'd say good-bye to Anna Marie and Connie, who'd ride off on their twin Schwinns, then we would walk home together. Or, to be more exact, I'd walk Wendy to the end of her street, Hawthorne Avenue, where she would wave and turn. There was something final about her wave—like a period at the end of a sentence that told me 'Stop right there.' I'd wave back and move on, trekking the added mile to Lazy Acres.

On Friday, I got a letter from Bailey. I still wrote twice a week, but her letters came less and less often. I wiggled my finger under the flap, unfolding two drawings and a letter. The first sketch was a portrait of Miss Billings, the town librarian. The second was of Oscar, who lived at the Beaver Creek feed store. Bailey and I had tried like the dickens to improve that dumb parrot's vocabulary, but he only said one thing: "Bottom of the ninth, bases loaded!"

I sat on the edge of my bed, holding Bailey's letter on my lap. *Dear Delores*, she wrote.

I miss you!

My eyes traveled the page, wondering where those other two *I miss you!*s had wandered off to. I turned the paper over, in case Bailey'd forgotten and written them on the backside instead. They were nowhere to be found. My stomach clenched as I read on.

*Our teacher, Miss Kittle, is getting married
next Saturday. Yesterday she talked about her
fiancé so much we missed social studies.*

*Next Saturday is also Becky Montgomery's
twelfth birthday. Her mama mailed scented
invitations to every girl in our class, asking us to a
fancy sit-down dinner. Mama's letting me borrow
her best Sunday dress for the occasion.*

*Did I tell you Becky knows French? She's teaching
me and Mary Stingpratt at recess. Well, that's all
the news. Bye for now. Or should I say, "Au revoir!"*

I folded Bailey's letter closed.

I knew everything was about to change between her and
me. I could feel it in my bones.

Staring down at the scar on my third finger, I touched the
raised lip of skin where I'd made a deep cut with Gramps's
penknife the day Bailey and me became blood sisters. Bailey'd been a big baby about the knife and insisted on one of
her mama's sewing needles to draw her blood.

Maybe that's why Bailey could replace me so quickly.
Her blood was close to the surface, just a pin stick away.
And mine went so deep it left a scar.

I stuffed Bailey's letter in the envelope.

The clock ain't stopped ticking in Beaver Creek, I told
myself. Life is going on without you.

First Frost

On Saturday morning the grass was blanketed with white gauze. "Holy moly," I said, rubbing sleep from my eyes. "What happened?"

Gram was scrubbing the floor with Mister Clean. "First frost. Pretty, ain't it?"

Pretty wouldn't have been my choice of words. *Dismal,* maybe.

I ate a bowl of Lucky Charms. Then I grabbed the furniture polish and a cloth rag and started down the hallway toward the bedrooms. I dusted and waxed while Gram vacuumed and scoured. After we were through, she poured us a tall glass of tea. Brother Thompson used to say Gram's sweet tea had more pucker power than you could shake a stick at. But I loved all the lemons she added and how the bitter blended with the sweet.

"Here's your allowance," Gram said, unfolding two one-dollar bills.

Like I said before, my allowance has been a dollar fifty since my eleventh birthday, so I wasn't near due for a raise. With Gramps gone, I probably wouldn't have dared hope for one for years.

"You want me to make change?" I asked.

Gram sipped her tea. "No need."

"Well, thanks." I picked up the bills before she could have second thoughts.

As I began to walk away, Gram reached for my hand. "Let's have lunch out."

"Out? As in, at a restaurant?"

Gram nodded.

Like I said, Gram can squeeze a quarter till the eagle squawks, so her giving me extra allowance and asking me out to lunch, both on the same day, was downright suspicious. I studied her face, making sure she wasn't an impostor. The woman staring back at me was Gram, all right.

"What's the special occasion?" I asked.

Gram hesitated. Finally, she said, "I accepted the offer on the house in Beaver Creek, Delores. They'll mail me a check for the deposit this week."

The room felt small, like the walls were closing in.

"I've been thinking," she continued. "Maybe you and me ought to get out more. Have some fun now and then."

"Fun?" I repeated. I didn't know the word was a part of Gram's vocabulary.

She nodded. "Woolworth's has got a Salisbury steak special I'd love to try. Is Woolworth's okay with you?"

"Well, sure, it sounds fine, but—"

"Okay, then." Gram started toward her room. "Gimme a little time to change."

We hadn't eaten out since Gramps passed on. Every Friday night we'd pile in the Bel Air and drive an hour each way so we could enjoy what Gramps promised was the best fish fry in Florida. I never asked him how he knew that because I took Gramps's word on everything. If he said the moon was made out of cottage cheese, the only question he'd get from me would be "Small curd or large?"

Gram and I sat at a booth by the window, watching as the shoppers dawdled past.

I ordered the fried chicken. It couldn't hold a candle to Cousin Effie's, but I enjoyed it all the same.

When Gram finished eating, she folded her napkin on her plate. "I forgot to tell you. I met Gwendolyn Parish's mama at the Cut-n-Curl. She's a regular, I hear."

I recalled my conversation with Billy. "What'd you think of her?" I asked.

Gram rubbed her stomach, like it was pestering her. "She spent every last minute boasting about her daughter. Gwendolyn this, Gwendolyn that . . ."

I shrugged. "That ain't so bad, is it?"

"The good Lord ain't fond of braggarts. Besides . . ." Gram's belly grumbled and she held her hand to her mouth, burping quietly. "Oh, dear, pardon me. That spicy gravy ain't agreeing with me."

I leaned forward. "Finish what you were saying, Gram. Besides what?"

"Well, it seems all that matters to Mrs. Parish is her daughter being top dog."

The waitress cleared our plates. Gram paid the check. "Let's go," she said, "I need something to ease this bellyache."

We wound up next door at Dreck's Drugs. Gram started toward the stomach remedies while I checked out the comic book display. Gramps used to buy me one every Saturday when he stopped at the store for cigars. I was thumbing through the latest issue of *Batman* when a pretty lady with sandy hair and dark eyes walked through the front door. Except she didn't just walk, she sashayed. My third-grade teacher, Miss Alderman, was out-and-out crazy about that word. She had people sashaying here and there all the time. As I watched that fancy-dressed lady breeze toward the back register with a straw hat she plucked off a mannequin, a sudden sorrow overcame me. I hadn't been on my Thinking Swing in over two months, but that didn't stop my brain from thinking, That lady could be your mama for all you know.

My ears prickled with heat. I glanced at the comic book, swallowing hard.

When I tried to return to the story, it was hard to concentrate. First, because of those melancholy mama thoughts. And second, because a sound in the distance distracted me. I heard a girl laughing and closed my finger on the page, glancing around. There was no one there. But as I flipped the book back open, the giggling started again.

I moved toward the sound, discovering a photo booth in the corner. The curtain was drawn, stirring with the movement inside. A white light exploded, escaping along the edges of the thick velvet cloth.

"Shoot!" a girl said. "I blinked!"

"Ow!" A second one snapped. "My hair, it's caught in your charm bracelet!"

"*Funny* on this shot," a third girl said, all bossy-like. "Pretend you saw Mrs. Meriwether's girdle hanging on the clothesline."

There was no doubt in my mind who those voices belonged to.

Another flash of light.

"Last picture—glamorous this time. Think Marilyn Monroe."

"How can I be glamorous when I've gotta pee?"

Flash!

The curtain parted. Out spilled Wendy, Connie, and Anna Marie, shrieking like the noon whistle.

Questions ricocheted through my brain: Why hadn't I been invited to their outing? Why wasn't I inside that photo booth with them, making cheesy faces and cutting up?

There was only one reason I could come up with. They'd decided I wasn't up to snuff for the Breck Girls. After all, I didn't have a mama and a daddy and live in a nice house with pristine sidewalks. What in Sam Hill was I thinking?

I decided I'd best make my getaway. I held the comic book in front of my face and darted down the toothpaste aisle.

"Delores," Wendy called, "is that you?"

My heart raced. I had my eye on the door.

"Delores," she called again, louder. "Wait up!"

I stuffed my hands in the pockets of my cutoffs, took a deep breath, and turned. "Yeah?"

Wendy was wearing lime green pedal pushers with a white Oxford shirt. She looked like she'd stepped out of a fashion magazine. "I've been calling you," she said.

I could taste the fried chicken coating creeping backwards, into my throat. "I—I'm sorry. I didn't hear you."

"Of *course* you didn't hear me. You weren't home."

"Home?" I repeated, confused.

Wendy rolled her eyes. "Yes. I got your phone number from the operator. I dialed it at least a dozen times, but there was no answer. Now I know why."

"Oh, yeah," I said, finally catching on. "Because I was here."

She smiled, pretend-swatting my arm. "We're going to see *Blackbeard's Ghost* at the matinee. We wanted to know if you'd like to come with us."

"Of course she would," Anna Marie said, joining us. Connie nodded, agreeing.

"I'll ask," I said, smiling so bright I could've melted a million first frosts.

Orange Crush

After the movie Anna Marie felt like swinging. I wasn't keen on the notion because (1) spending five days a week at school was plenty for me, and (2) my bottom hadn't touched a swing since I'd said good-bye to my Thinking Swing. But there's one thing I'd learned from the get-go. What Anna Marie says, sticks.

On our way we passed Lakeville Records, where I'd bought my Beatles 45, which I still hadn't found the nerve to ask Gram to play on her phonograph. A song by Diana Ross and the Supremes spilled through the open door.

Wendy stopped on a dime, shouting, "I love this song!" She held up a candy bar she'd bought, pretending it was a microphone. "Stop," she sang, thrusting her palm forward, "in the naaaaaame of love . . ."

Wendy had *stage presence*, all right. And she didn't need a curtain call to conjure it. She motioned us closer. We flanked her sides like the Supremes, swaying our hips, pointing at an imaginary audience each time she sang "*Stop!*"

People gathered to watch. First there were three smiling faces, then seven, then ten. After a dozen, I plumb lost track. When the song ended, everyone clapped. "Encore!" someone yelled.

Now, I have never been the showy type. Gram claims it's 'cause of my being born breech, that I was opposed to showing my face from day one. But, standing beside Wendy and Anna Marie and Connie, hamming it up, I felt like a brand-new person. Maybe having friends gave me confidence. All I know is this: When the song was over and the crowd applauded, I was downright tickled that all that fussing and carrying on was for us.

We joined hands and took a bow. Then Wendy gave a quick tug, pulling us behind her down the street.

Connie glanced over her shoulder, pouting. "Why can't we sing another song?"

"Rule number one," Wendy said. "Always leave your audience wanting more."

Connie shot back, "I think that's a stupid ru—"

"Never mind that," Anna Marie interrupted, elbowing us toward Woolworth's. "Let's get a soda, my treat." We walked around back to the pop machine. Anna Marie dropped several coins in the slot, pulling out four Orange Crushes.

I held my bottle forward. "Cheers!" I said. "To Diana Ross!"

"To the Supremes!" Wendy added.

We all clinked and sipped, staring out at the parking lot. Wendy pointed at a shiny blue Lincoln Continental. "When I'm older, that's the kind of car I want. A nice four-door sedan. My father says big cars are the safest if you're ever in an accident."

"There's my dream car," Connie said, pointing to a Pontiac GTO.

Anna Marie tipped the neck of her bottle toward a fire-red Impala. "That's mine." She turned to face me. "How about you, Delores? Where's your dream car?"

How could I explain that we already owned it? And the only thing I dreamed about was taking the lousy FOR SALE sign off its windshield. "It ain't here," I told her.

Anna Marie said, "Describe it, then."

"It's a convertible."

"What color?"

I took a long swig of my Crush. The soda fizz tickled my nose and I stifled a burp. "Turquoise and white," I answered, and I should've quit right there. But something made me add one of Gramps's favorite features. "With wide white-wall tires."

Anna Marie chuckled. "Whitewall tires haven't been in style for years."

"Maybe Delores likes antique cars," Wendy said.

"Oh, *please.*" Connie waved her hand. "My dad drags my brother and me to antique car shows all the time. They are sooo boring. He looks under the hood and asks the owner how much horsepower the engine has and whether it's a V-5 or V-6 or—"

"Actually," I said, "there's no such thing as a V-5."

"Oh," Connie said. "Really?"

I nodded. "The number after the V tells you how many cylinders the car's got—usually it's four, six, or eight. But it's always an even number."

"Thinking of becoming a mechanic?" Anna Marie quipped.

"I like knowing a little bit about a lot of things," I told her.

"If you're such a smarty-pants," she said, "why do you say *ain't* all the time?"

Gram claims there are people we naturally lock horns with. If I wasn't careful, that could easily happen between Anna Marie Armstrong and me. I looked away. "That's just how people talk where I come from."

Anna Marie batted her eyelashes. "And where exactly is that again?"

"Truce!" Wendy called, stepping between us. "The last person to the swings buys the Cracker Jacks."

A dime was all I had left from the movie theater. And ten cents wouldn't buy one box of Cracker Jacks, let alone four. So I ditched my half-empty Crush in the trash, and I was up and out of there, pronto.

Lavender

I leaned against the jungle gym, catching my breath. A breeze blew and flame-colored leaves danced past. I'd seen pictures of autumn—trees red as cherry lollipops, skies so bright they looked painted on—but I'd never seen the real thing.

Wendy panted toward me. "How'd you . . . get here . . . so fast?"

I shrugged and followed her to the swings. There were eight of them in all—two big and six small. The smaller ones were fine for the little kids, but no self-respecting sixth-grader would so much as look at them.

Wendy plunked down, pumping her legs. Anna Marie and Connie appeared across the playground. Anna Marie held her stomach. Connie pinched a crick in her side.

I stood there, staring at the second swing.

Wendy swooped back and forth. "What are you waiting for?" she asked me.

I backed into the swing, leaning against the seat—not a wooden seat, but a cold, black, rubbery one that felt strange and unfamiliar. I closed my fingers around the chains. My hands ached for the prickly tickle of the rope on my old swing.

I rested my weight on the seat. It folded around me, pinching my knees together. I was suddenly convinced something terrible would happen. The chains might snap. Or the U-shaped seat might deform my hips. Some penance for the disservice I was doing to the memory of my Thinking Swing.

I was considering giving up that swing to Anna Marie or Connie, even though I'd beat them to it, fair and square, when, out of nowhere, one of Gramps's old sayings popped into my head. It was as if he was right there, talking to me.

If you can't run with the big dogs, stay under the dang porch.

Well, I thought, I've never been one for porch-dawdling. So I drew a deep breath and blew it out. Silently, I counted down from five. On one, I leaned back. Dug my heels into the dirt. Lifted off. Pumped like I meant business.

And nothing bad happened. In fact, it felt nice being on a swing again, even a dumb rubber and chain swing. My stomach lurched each time I dipped toward the grass. Wendy and I zipped back and forth, a pair of giant scissors, clipping the air between us.

I arched back, staring up at the sky. It was a brilliant turquoise, the same shade of blue as Gramps's Chevy. I glanced at Wendy. "What's your favorite color?" I asked her.

"Certainly not yellow," she said. "My mother claims it's a power color, so that's what she picked for my room. I feel like I'm trapped inside a box of marshmallow Peeps."

I smiled. "Okay. Yellow's out of the race."

I was surprised Wendy had to think about her answer. I was sure a favorite color was something you were born with, like a nose or a belly button.

"Definitely not pink," she continued. "My room was pink before it was yellow and I hated *that* color almost as much."

I was relieved to hear that. "What would you paint your room if *you* got to pick?"

"Oh, right. Like my mother would let me decide."

"Pretend. What color?"

Wendy squinted at the house next door to school. The steps were lined with potted mums. I was surprised they looked so peppy after the frost we'd had.

"That color," Wendy said, tipping her chin toward the plants.

"Light purple?"

"Yes." Wendy nodded. "Lavender."

Wendy was right. Lavender did sound better than light purple. I decided to add it to my Favorite Words list. I didn't have any L-words.

"I'll never get to paint my room lavender." Wendy sighed. "My mother took a psychology course in college. She says purple is the favorite color of lunatics."

Another L-word. "Really?"

"I don't believe her, though. My father's brother, my uncle Ray, is a lunatic. He lives in a state mental hospital in New York, and his favorite color is white. He'll eat only white foods because he thinks all colored foods are poisonous. So there goes that theory."

"Well"—I stretched my leg out, tapping the tip of a branch—"I say you can like any old color you please."

"Well"—Wendy pointed her toe, touching the same branch—"I say you're right!" She let go of her chains, leaping through the air, the tails of her shirt flapping at her sides. She landed hard on both heels. "My favorite color," she called, flinging her arms out, "is *lavender*!"

Anna Marie and Connie turned to stare. That didn't stop Wendy. She twirled in circles, shouting, "Lavender, lavender, lavender!"

I smiled, thinking, I'm sure glad Wendy's mama ain't here to see this, 'cause she's carrying on like a lunatic.

Gone Fishin'

Gram decided it was high time we became churchgoing citizens again. "The Lord don't take kindly to lollygaggers," she explained. So that next morning we set off for the Holy Hope Baptist Church in Lakeville. Afterwards, we had brunch at Hollis and Effie's, and I ate enough for three people. Gram says I'm like Gramps in that regard—I can eat anything and still remain skinny as a rail.

Gram stayed on with Cousin Effie. They had a new cinnamon-apple cake recipe they were both eager to try. I headed next door to change my clothes. I intended to stretch out on the warm grass with a good book, enjoying what folks in Ohio called Indian summer, when, after the first frost, the days turn hot again. Or what Ohioans *think* hot is. If they ain't ever been to Florida, they're just plain fooling themselves.

On my way to the fridge for a soda I heard a rap at our door. I peered outside, and there stood Billy Applegate, his newspaper bag slung over one shoulder.

"Hey," I said.

"Hey," he said back.

"My grandma's next door if you're collecting for the paper."

"She's paid up till the end of next week," Billy said.

A fly landed on the screen between us. "What's up, then?" I asked him.

Billy lifted the bag off his shoulder. He wadded it into a ball, stuffing it beneath one arm. "I just finished my route and was thinking maybe you'd wanna do something."

"Like what?"

Billy shrugged. "Play catch, scare up some frogs, I don't know."

I narrowed my eyes at him. "By any chance, do you like to fish?"

"Hell, yeah! But I almost never get to 'cause my big brother Clive nabs the pole first. Except when he's got a girlfriend, then he could care less about fishing 'cause he's busy doing other things." Billy blushed. "Last summer I caught a two-pound trout."

"Really?" I asked. "Where?"

Billy motioned toward the field abutting the dirt road. "You cut across there and keep going till you come to these woods, about a mile or so out. You weave your way through, probably another mile. Then you'll see a giant stone wall. On the other side's a stream. Hardly anybody knows about it. . . . I'll show you sometime, if you want."

My heart was beating double-time. "How about right now? I'll have to ask my grandma first, but I'm sure she'll say it's okay."

Billy frowned. "Sorry. Clive's between girlfriends. He took off with the pole."

"Wait here," I said, hurrying down the hall to Gram's ironing room. I reached into the closet and removed Gramps's and my fishing rods. Then I grabbed the tackle box.

When Billy saw me, his mouth fell open. "You got your own poles? Two of 'em?"

"This one's my grandpa's," I said, holding tight, "but you can use mine."

Billy's eyes grew wide. "Seriously?"

"Seriously." I opened the door and slipped past him. "You wait here. I'm heading next door to ask Gram if I can go." I turned halfway between our tiny yard and Cousin Effie's. "By the way," I added, grinning, "since I saw to the poles, you're in charge of the bait."

I followed Billy along the path he'd described. Finally, he motioned toward a low, flat rock, parked beside a small, bubbling stream. I sat beside Billy, noticing he had more freckles on the left side of his face than the right. "It's peaceful here," I said.

"Yeah, nobody bugs you." Billy slapped a mosquito. "Well, except the bugs." He laughed at his own joke.

I glanced around. "How'd you find this place?"

"Last summer our cat Scamper went missing. I must've walked twenty miles looking for her. I was about to give up when I heard her mewing. She was stuck in that tree." He tipped his chin toward a giant elm. "If it weren't for her running off, I never would've known this was here."

I nodded, thinking how life is like that. One thing

happens on account of something else, and so on and so on. Like a long line of dominoes.

We adjusted the worms on our hooks and cast our lines in the water.

After that we were quiet. The kind of bone-deep quiet me and Bailey used to share at the swamp. And as the water *blub-blub*ed over the shiny moss-covered stones, and the sun squeezed through the trees, spattering dabs of light on the gray-green water, I thought, Bailey would like this place, too. I breathed out slowly, letting go of so much more than just air.

"Hey," Billy called, "I got something!" He rocked back, reeling in his line. "It's big. *Real* big!" His behind scooted this way and that across the flat rock. "Get ready. I'm bringing 'er in!" With one quick jerk, he whipped his line out of the water.

Billy's catch dangled before us.

Except it wasn't a fish.

I bit my cheeks to keep from laughing. "It's a work boot," I said, flat out.

"Aw, nerts!" Billy untangled the shoelace from his line. He tipped the boot upside down, emptying the water in the stream. Then he set it between us on the rock.

"Makes a nice centerpiece," I said, yanking up a handful of asters, sticking them inside the opening.

"Now all we need is some food to go with it." Billy eyed the lunch Gram had packed us. He'd tried to talk her out of it, after she came next door to meet him. He told her he planned to catch several bluegills and cook them over a fire, but Gram insisted. "Just in case the fish ain't biting," she said.

"Whaddaya suppose we got?" Billy asked, looking as hungry as he was curious.

"One way to find out." I reached inside the bag, pulling out two paper napkins, two cans of soda, and two sandwiches. "Smells like tuna," I said, sniffing the wax paper.

Billy moaned. "Did she do that on purpose?"

"Do what?"

"You know, give us tuna—in case we didn't catch a fish of our own?"

"It *must* be a coincidence," I said. Because a coincidence was easier to fathom than Gram playing anything even resembling a practical joke.

Still, as I bit into my sandwich, I did have to scratch my head and wonder.

Dry Toast and Grapefruit

On Monday morning I was unwrapping my dessert, one of Cousin Effie's fudge brownies, which I'd decided to eat on my way to school, when Wendy called, "Delores! Wait up!"

She was wearing a navy blue sailor dress. Her tights were bright white, and her patent-leather shoes gleamed like they'd been polished five seconds ago.

When she caught up, I broke the brownie in two. "Here," I said, "want half?"

Wendy glanced at the chocolate square. "No, thank you."

"Big breakfast?"

"Try dry toast and half a grapefruit. But only after thirty minutes of exercising with Jack La Lanne."

"Wow. Do you do that every morning?"

"No, I just started today."

"But, why?"

Wendy sighed. "My mother made me report everything I ate and drank before, during, and after the movie on Saturday—popcorn, Raisinets, Three Musketeers bar, Orange Crush, Cracker Jacks, the candy necklace. She added everything up on her calorie counter. She claims I consumed close to two thousand calories in nonnutritious food."

"But everybody eats that kind of stuff at the movie theater."

"I told you, Delores, I'm not everybody." Her voice dropped. "Nobody wants to see a *fat* baton twirler."

"Wendy, if you're fat, I'm Roy Rogers!"

"Roy who?"

"Somebody my grandpa liked. All I'm trying to say is, you're not fat."

"Well, my mother sees things differently. She has a new nickname for me. Gwendolyn the Corpulent."

Wendy had me stumped. "Corpulent?"

"Obese."

"Well, that's not a very nice name for somebody's mother to be—"

"Delores," she interrupted. "Eating all that stuff on Saturday was a mistake. And mistakes have consequences. Mistakes cost performers success."

"Wendy," I said, "what are you talking about?"

"Semifinals for the state twirling competition are in Columbus in three weeks. My mother paid a dress designer a fortune to create my costume. It fit me fine a month ago, but now it's too tight."

"What are you gonna do?"

Wendy wiped away a tear—roughly, like she was scrubbing dirt off her sleeve. "Whatever my mother says," she answered.

Becoming Dee-Dee

Wendy and I were the first to arrive at our lunch table. Anna Marie and Connie's teacher, Miss Perkins, held their class back. Dinky Nolan and Elmer Tangiers had gotten in trouble during the air raid drill we'd practiced that morning. After every sixth-grader faced the wall, knelt, and bent forward, covering their heads, Dinky and Elmer got the bright idea of blowing phony fart noises into the crooks of their arms. So their entire class was still in the room listening to a very loud lecture on how to behave during a drill.

Wendy opened her lunchbox. She bit the end off a carrot stick, made a face, and tossed it back in the bag. Then she unscrewed her thermos, poured chicken broth into the cup, and dipped a dry half sandwich.

"That doesn't look very appetizing," I said.

She stared at the soggy bread. "You're telling me."

Anna Marie came out of nowhere, slamming her lunchbox on the table. "Boys are so immature. I'm glad we don't have to sit through the movie with them."

"What movie?" I asked.

"The sex education film," she answered matter-of-factly, like she used the word *sex* a dozen times every day. "There are two versions—one for the boys and one for the girls. We watch them in separate rooms. Thank God."

"I heard Elmer plans on faking a headache during the boys' movie," Connie said. "And instead of going to the nurse, he'll sneak to where they're showing our movie so he can peek through the window."

Anna Marie flipped her braids back. "That doesn't surprise me."

When the bell rang, we dumped our trash and hurried toward the playground door.

The blacktop glistened in the sun. The heat rose up through the macadam, warming the soles of my Keds. Anna Marie stepped in front of me. She reached in her pocket and pulled out two rubber bands. "Your hair could use some help," she said, looping them around her wrist. "I'll braid it for you."

I wasn't keen on the notion, but like I said, nobody argues with Anna Marie.

"Over here," she said, leading the way toward the shade, far enough from the playground so we couldn't hear someone sing "I see London, I see France, I see someone's underpants" every time a girl crossed the monkey bars.

I sat on the prickly grass and Anna Marie knelt behind me. I could feel her fingernail drag my scalp, divvying my hair into two even clumps.

Wendy and Connie started toward the swings. I watched Wendy hold her skirt in place as she slid backwards onto the seat, carefully tucking the fabric beneath her legs before taking off. I thought of her welts again, and of how bad I wanted to know how she got them. But I couldn't just come out and ask.

After Anna Marie snapped the second rubber band in place, she stood and inspected her work. Her braids were long, nearly reaching her waist. Mine were short, barely clearing my chin.

"You should grow your hair long," she said. "You'd look prettier."

I didn't bother to inform her that looking pretty wasn't my number one concern in life. "I'll think about it," I said.

"Please do. Now"—her eyes narrowed—"what can we do about your name?"

"What's wrong with my name?" I asked. I wasn't crazy about it, either. But that's not the point.

"Delores is too old-fashioned. We need to come up with something . . ." She glanced around, like the answer dangled from a tree branch. ". . . snappier."

I opened my mouth to speak, then closed it. Sure, Anna Marie was as full of wind as a corn-eating horse, but I had to admit, I *was* enjoying myself with the Breck Girls. I'd never had more than one friend at a time, let alone made friends with any popular girls. So I did what anybody in my shoes would've done. I turned to Anna Marie and said, "Whatcha got in mind?"

"I'm thinking." She folded her arms. "How about Dell? No, I don't like it."

I waited.

"Delly?" Anna Marie shook her head. "Scratch that. It reminds me of where you buy salami."

"I know!" Anna Marie smiled. "Dee-Dee. Yes, Dee-Dee's your new Official Nickname. If it's all right with you, of course."

I turned the sound round and round in my brain.

Dee-Dee . . .

Dee-Dee . . .

I decided it wasn't half bad. "Sure," I answered. "Why not?"

Words have power, Gramps used to say. *All the power of a solid left hook.* And, boy, was he right. Each day, as Wendy nibbled on her dry half sandwich to avoid becoming Gwendolyn the

Corpulent, I struggled with my new name, too. I'd only ever had one nickname—Itch—and the whole time I'd been called that, I never once wondered how I ought to behave. Being me came naturally. But now I wondered constantly. Becoming Dee-Dee was like breaking in a new pair of shoes.

Every day I let Anna Marie braid my hair. And the following week, I agreed to a coat of her nail polish—a clear shade so Gram wouldn't notice. Next, she talked me into shaving my legs. After school one day, while Gram was still working, I hunted for Gramps's electric razor, which Gram had saved since it worked like a charm for removing sweater nubs. I gave my fuzzy legs a good once-over. Three days later, my shins felt like porcupines, and I had to shave them again, so I didn't see much sense in the act.

But Anna Marie thought it was important to shave. And to wear nail polish. And to have a "fashionable" hairstyle, as she called it.

I was becoming somebody she approved of.

I was becoming Dee-Dee.

Doors Open, Doors Close

Wendy lost six pounds in two weeks. On the Friday before her state twirling competition, we met at my locker after school. "Looks like we all survived," she said. I knew she was referring to the movie. During the last several days, all of our classes had watched it.

I stacked my books on the shelf and reached for my lunchbox. "It's hard to believe all that stuff's gonna happen to us." I glanced down at my flat chest. "And soon."

"Hopefully not too soon. I can finally fit into my costume again."

On the way to Wendy's locker, I asked, "When are you leaving for Columbus?"

"Six in the morning. The competition starts at nine. They expect over a hundred entries, and they only pick ten for the finals."

"Have you ever made it to the finals before?" I asked.

Wendy nodded. "Twice. I came in ninth two years ago and seventh last year."

"You were the seventh-best baton twirler in the whole state? That's good!"

"Not really. Only the top five get trophies. And only the winner gets a cash prize. Anyway . . ." Wendy waved her hand, changing the subject. "I was wondering if you'd like to come to my house after school on Monday."

"What about your dance lessons?"

"The studio's closed on Monday, remember?"

I pictured Mrs. Parish's cold stare. "Are you sure it's all right with your mother?"

"Dee-Dee, you *really* weren't listening. She has her hair appointment that day. My dad will be home, though. He takes Monday afternoons off. It's his worst day for sales.

Everyone's recuperating from their weekend cocktail parties."

I'd never known anybody who went to a cocktail party. Gram and Gramps used to invite Opal and Ed Purdy over for cards and Genesee beer. I don't suppose that counted.

Wendy leaned close, whispering, "If you say yes, I'll show you the supplies for our monthlies." She shrugged. "Unless you've already seen them."

Gram had never mentioned owning anything even resembling the contraptions they showed us in the movie. If she did, she kept them well hidden.

We walked down the hall toward the door. "Are we on for Monday?" she asked.

I paused, thinking how *Dee-Dee* would answer her question. As I started down the stairs, my lunchbox swinging at my side, I said, "I think you can pencil me in."

I stopped at the mailboxes on my way home. Leaning against the electric light bill was a letter from Bailey. Finally. I hadn't heard from her since she'd told me about Becky Montgomery's birthday party. I was long overdue for some news.

When I wiggled my finger under the flap, a photograph toppled out. A group of girls, their lips and cheeks painted rose-petal pink, were gathered around a giant three-layer cake topped with twinkling candles. I recognized most of them—Fern Harper and Betty Lou Trumbull and Carolyn Beaumont, who'd been in my fifth-grade class, and snotty Mary Stinky-pants and poor Nettie Bonham, whose daddy was crippled with polio. But the girl in the middle, the one wearing a tiara, was a stranger to me. Not to Bailey, though. Bailey leaned into her side, smiling so widely I could see the tooth she'd chipped the day we decided to make parachutes out of bed sheets and jump out her second-story window.

I unfolded Bailey's letter.

Dear Delores, she began.

My heart sank. Where the three *I miss you!*s used to go, Bailey had skipped a line, then continued:

> *Mama's as big as a barn now. Her doctor*
> *says the twins will definitely be here for Christmas.*
> *Daddy found two baby bassinets at the annual*
> *church rummage sale and spray-painted them*
> *yellow so it won't matter if Mama has boys or girls.*
> *I'm sorry I'm not sending a drawing this time.*
> *I've been busy helping Becky paint a mural in her*
> *family's rec room. But hopefully you'll like the*
> *picture from her birthday party. Mrs. Montgomery*
> *gave all of us an Avon makeover. She told me I*
> *have "highly defined cheekbones"* and could*
> *maybe be a fashion model someday.*
> *Well, time to babysit AGAIN! Je dois y aller.*
> *(That's French for "I must go!")*
>
> Your friend, Bailey
>
> **Mrs. Montgomery's exact words*

I crammed the picture in the envelope, stomping the rest of the way home. When my toes touched our driveway, my mood went from bad to worse. The FOR SALE sign on Gramps's Bel Air was flipped over. Lettered across its backside in bold black letters was the word SOLD. I glanced at my watch. I had two full hours to stew in my juices before Gram came home, so I ran next door to Cousin Effie's and pounded on the door.

"C'mon in," she hollered.

Hollis was asleep in his recliner. I zipped past him into the kitchen, where Cousin Effie stood shaping ground beef into patties.

"Something wrong?" she asked me.

I crossed my arms. "What do you know about Gramps's car?"

"Some fella came by and told Eunice it'd be perfect for his wife to—"

"No!" I yelled. "That car ain't perfect for anybody except Gram and me."

Cousin Effie offered a sympathetic look that made her look constipated. "But Eunice don't drive, Delores. Wouldn't you rather see it appreciated by somebody who—"

"I reckon I wouldn't!" I blurted out, waking Hollis in the next room.

The kitchen was suddenly silent. "I made a pecan pie this morning," Cousin Effie said. "How about a slice with some vanilla ice cream on top?"

"I'm sorry," I said, starting toward the door. "I ain't got much of an appetite."

At half past five, Gram arrived. She slipped off her shoes, and they clunked to the floor like bricks. "Effie stopped me. She said you came by, upset about the car."

I reached for the plates to set the table. "Yes, ma'am," I answered.

She walked to the refrigerator, removing a tuna-noodle casserole. "Try to understand. Your grandpa's car isn't gonna do either of us any good just sitting there."

Little did she know. I could hop in the back and make the whole world disappear.

I grabbed the silverware next. Gram had a superstition: If you dropped a knife, a man would visit you. If you dropped a fork, a woman would show up; a spoon, a child. "When's the man coming for the car?" I asked, holding extra tight to the knife.

"Mr. Maxwell couldn't say. He'll be out of town on business till next month. Sometime after that, I s'pose. He left me a deposit to hold it."

I set the silverware in its place. Clearly, there was nothing more to say.

Fear

I spent most of my weekend moping around, waiting for Monday to arrive.

When Wendy's father's car pulled to the curb at school that morning, I flew over, lickety-split. As soon as Wendy stepped out, I asked, "Did you make the semifinals?"

"Yes!" she answered.

We jumped up and down, yipping like two silly ninnies.

The day dragged on and on, till finally the dismissal bell rang. Anna Marie and Connie pedaled off on their bikes while Wendy and I took our usual route. Except I didn't pause at Wendy's corner and keep walking. This time I stuck by her side.

I recognized her father's car, parked in the driveway of a large two-story house. Huge jack-o'-lanterns edged the steps, and cornstalks flanked the door.

Wendy led the way inside. "Come on," she said. "I'll introduce you to my dad. He's probably in the library."

At the end of a long hallway, Wendy took a left, and I followed her.

Dark wooden shelves lined the walls from floor to ceiling. One half was filled with books, their leather bindings arranged from tallest to shortest. The other was lined with trophies, each engraved with Wendy's name. My mouth dropped open as I walked from one to the next. "How many of these have you got?" I asked her.

"One hundred and nineteen, the last time my mother counted."

I noticed a picture on a far wall—a large oval portrait in a fancy gold frame. I stepped closer. A girl in a tiara and tutu balanced on the tips of her toes, smiling as she clutched a dozen roses. She looked like Wendy, only older. "Who's that?" I asked.

"My mother when she was fourteen," Wendy said. "She'd just finished the summer season with the Lakeville Ballet."

I recalled Wendy's mother, limping across the fairgrounds.

As if she'd read my mind, Wendy said, "The portrait was taken before her accident." She reached for an album and flipped it open, removing a photo of the same girl, slightly older and heavier, and definitely a whole lot sadder. Below her checkered skirt a long scar stretched from her knee to her ankle. "This was her after the accident."

I squinted at the photo, then back at the dancer with the roses. "What happened?"

"When my mother was in high school, she liked this boy named Danny. One day, he offered her a ride on his bike. My mother was sitting on his handlebars when Danny's tire hit a rut. Her foot caught in the spokes and she heard a loud *snap* and went flying. When she landed, a bone was poking right through her shin. The doctor said it was broken in five places. She kept going back for more surgery, but her leg didn't heal properly." Wendy stared wistfully at the portrait. "My mother wasn't ever able to dance again. That's why she wants me to have all the opportunities she missed."

Wendy sighed, starting back down the hall. When we got to the living room, she clicked on a lamp.

A man in a recliner sat up, the footrest collapsing with a snap. "Hey, Pickle," he said in a groggy voice.

Wendy crossed the room, hugging him full-force, just like I used to hug Gramps. A jab stabbed me. I drew a deep breath and looked away.

Wendy turned, leaning on the arm of his recliner. "Daddy, I'd like you to meet my new friend, Delores Colchester. We call her Dee-Dee. She moved here from Florida, and she has an accent. Say something, Dee-Dee."

I felt like a circus animal. I shoved my hands in my pockets and recited something Gramps used to say. "Where I come from, it's hot enough to fry an egg on the sidewalk."

The corners of his lips turned up. Gramps would've called it an honest smile.

Wendy hurried to my side, looping her arm through mine. "I'm going to make us some popcorn," she told him. "Then we're going to visit in my room."

Her father's face grew serious. "Is popcorn a snack your mother allows, Pickle?"

"Yes, Daddy," she answered, pulling me behind her, toward the kitchen. "As long as I don't use butter."

Bringing Wendy the Ocean

I'd never seen anybody cook on an electric range before. Wendy pushed a button and the rings lit up, glowing like a bright red bull's-eye. She put a kettle on the burner, spooned in Crisco, and added popcorn. Glancing back toward the living room, she held a finger to her lips, opened the refrigerator, then grabbed a stick of butter.

"Wendy," I whispered, "maybe you shouldn't do that."

"I'll only take a smidge off the end," she whispered back, setting the stick beside the burner. "No one will ever notice."

Wendy added a lid and shook the kettle. Hot oil hissed against the sides. A kernel popped, and then a second. My mouth watered from the smell.

"Oops," Wendy said. "Almost forgot to check my chores list." A small paper was tacked to the fridge with a magnet. Wendy read it, mumbling, "Soap is already added . . . don't forget to empty it afterwards. . . ." She walked to where I leaned against the counter and reached behind me, turning a mysterious dial.

I didn't pay any mind to what she'd done till a sudden noise startled me—a jarring *vroom!* followed by a loud *whoosh*ing sound. I jumped away fast. "What the—?"

Wendy stifled a laugh. She pointed at the beige door built into the cupboards. "It's the dishwasher, Dee-Dee."

I'd never seen one of those before either. Gram said the only dishwasher we needed was made by L and R, as in left and right hands. I leaned backwards against the warm door, deciding I liked the sound. It reminded me of the ocean—each hard, wet slosh followed by a small airy pause. I recalled the time Gramps drove us to Hollywood Beach and we convinced Gram to remove her shoes and walk through the sand. She made a face as her toes sunk in. "Hot as blazes," she snapped, fixing not to like it one bit. But when a wave rolled toward her, splashing her calves, Gram looked downright contented.

The dishwasher clattered to a halt, and I bolted upright. I was so lost in my thoughts I hadn't even noticed the corn had stopped popping.

Wendy turned, facing me. "What's wrong?" she said. "You look sad."

The dishwasher groaned back to life, churning up a storm in my middle. Before I could say Jiminy Cricket, my eyes filled. I swiped my nose. "You'll laugh," I said.

"No, I won't. Promise."

"The sound of the dishwasher, it, um, it made me miss the ocean."

Wendy kept her word. She didn't laugh. "I've never been to the ocean."

"You haven't?" I'd have guessed she'd been everywhere there was to go.

Wendy shook her head no.

The dishwasher sloshed and swooshed.

Wendy closed her eyes.

"What're you doing?" I asked her.

"I'm picturing the ocean. Quick, before the cycle ends, describe it to me."

"Well, the color of the water depends on what the weather's like."

"It's sunny."

"Okay. The ocean's bright blue, just like the sky. And the sand's hot on your bare feet. So you'll need to hurry to the water."

She nodded. "All right."

"The water's cooler than the sand. Still, it's bathwater warm."

The toes of Wendy's shoes wiggled up and down. "Mmm," she said.

"You'll feel the tide," I continued. "First the waves roll toward you. Then the water slips away, out to sea, and the sand gets sucked right out from under your feet. It's strange—like the earth is moving—but you get used to it."

"What else?"

I closed my eyes, too. "Oh, yeah, the seagulls. You hear them everywhere, kind of like"—I tried to imitate their call—"*caaaaw, caaaw.* Sometimes they swoop so low you can see every feather. Once one got so close, he pooped on my shoulder."

Wendy grinned. "What's it smell like?"

"Seagull poop?"

"No." She giggled. "The ocean."

"Like tanning oil and dead fish and . . ." I inhaled deeply, but I was smelling something else besides the ocean. I opened my eyes and glanced toward the stove. The butter had melted into a wide pool. "Wendy, sorry"—I tapped her—"but we've got a mess to clean up."

Wendy's yellow walls, what you could see of them, were plastered with dog posters. Her bed was filled with dogs, too—cloth dogs, crocheted dogs, stuffed dogs.

My eyes landed on a large framed photo on Wendy's dresser, a picture of a brown-haired pooch with big floppy ears. "What's his name?" I asked.

Wendy lifted a stuffed beagle off her rocker so I could sit. She leaned against her bed, setting the popcorn between us. "Cocoa Puffs," she answered. "I named him after the cereal, because he was the exact same color. I called him Cocoa, for short."

"Called? What happened to him?"

"He died when I was in fourth grade."

"Oh," I said. "I'm sorry."

Wendy pointed to a round cushion in the corner. "That was Cocoa's bed. The only time my mother let Cocoa come into my bed with me was in first grade, after I had my tonsils out." Wendy shrugged. "I guess she felt sorry for me."

"Think you'll ever get another dog?" I asked.

Wendy grabbed a handful of popcorn, chewing hard. "Probably not. My mother says dogs are too much responsibility, especially with my classes and traveling around." Wendy reached behind her and held up a stuffed Dalmatian—"now I collect artificial dogs. This is Bruce, my favorite. My father bought him for me in Germany, on a business trip." Wendy waved Bruce's fuzzy paw. "Look, Dee-Dee, he's saying hello. Aren't you going to say hi back?"

I didn't want to be a spoilsport, so I said, "Hey, Bruce, how's life treating you?"

She held Bruce in front of her face and dropped her voice several octaves. "Not so great. I've got fleas, my rear end itches, and I have to pee."

I grabbed a brown sock dog, bouncing him up and down on my knee. Out of the corner of my mouth, I said, "I've gotta pee, too."

Wendy laughed. She held Bruce to her ear, burying his snout in her curls. "*Psst—Psst—Psst,*" he pretend-whispered in her ear. Wendy nodded her head. Then she turned to face me. "Bruce wants to know if you'll come back *next* Monday."

Bruce's eyes were shiny and round, gold as butterscotch drops.

"Sure," I told him, "I'd love to."

Missing Wendy

I waited for Wendy outside school the next morning, but her father's car never showed up. When I passed Wendy's classroom, her desk was empty. At lunch, I stood beside our table, staring down at the spot where she usually sat.

In a snippy-sounding voice, Anna Marie asked me, "Aren't you going to sit down?" Her moods were as change-able as Florida weather during hurricane season. I could tell from the get-go the forecast was looking mighty stormy.

I held my skirt in place and swung my leg over the bench—something I'd learned to do as easily and gracefully as Wendy. I glanced inside Anna Marie's lunchbox. Tucked in one corner was a pair of dark-framed spectacles, folded behind a large shiny apple. "Hey," I said, pointing, "what are those?"

"They're called *glasses*," she quipped. "Don't they have those in Florida?"

I thought of Bernice Dibbs, the school bully back in Beaver Creek, and how much I'd love to sic her on Anna Marie. "Yes, as a matter of fact, they do. Except in Florida people wear them on their faces. They don't much care if their fruit has twenty-twenty vision."

Connie giggled.

Anna Marie shot her a look.

I sat down, emptying my Lassie lunchbox. "Has anyone seen Wendy?"

"She's out sick," Connie answered.

"With what?" I asked.

"Who knows?" Anna Marie shrugged, picking the lettuce off her sandwich.

"What Anna Marie means," Connie explained, "is that Wendy's absent more than most kids. Poor thing, last year she had mumps, the flu, *and* an ear infection."

"She had her tonsils out, too," Anna Marie added.

"Hang on," I said. "Wendy had her tonsils out in first grade."

"Dee-Dee"—Anna Marie pointed a potato stick at me—"How would you know? You weren't even here."

"Because Wendy told me. It was the one time Wendy's mother let her dog, Cocoa, sleep on her bed."

Connie turned to Anna Marie. "Wendy has a dog?"

"Not anymore," I said. "He died. But Wendy keeps his picture in her room on—"

"I have no idea what picture you're talking about," Anna Marie interrupted. She closed her lunchbox, loudly, like she was shutting down the conversation, too.

"Didn't you notice it when you . . . ?"

Anna Marie and Connie exchanged glances. There was a long, uncomfortable silence.

Connie peeled the paper off a Tootsie Roll. She slid a

second one to Anna Marie and a third one to me. "Wendy's hard to visit," Connie said. "Either she's not home because she's taking dance classes—or if she is at home and decides to invite you in, she's a nervous wreck because her mother's right there, listening to everything." Connie shuddered. "She gives me the creeps."

The recess bell rang. Anna Marie stood quickly, lunchbox in hand, marching toward the playground door.

Connie watched her walk away. "Dee-Dee, she's jealous, that's all. Anna Marie never saw the picture in Wendy's room because she never got farther than the living room. Neither did I. You should consider yourself lucky. Now, come on." Connie motioned toward the exit. "Let's go find Anna Marie."

Loquacious

Wendy was out of school the next day too. I was beginning to feel like Anna Marie and Connie's third wheel. I spent most of my time nodding, half listening to them talk about something I couldn't care less about. So during recess, when they started toward the swings, I decided to sit on the sidelines, reading a library book.

The mid-October air was cool. I found the perfect spot

to relax, on a thick tuft of grass the sun had warmed up nicely. I finished one chapter and was about to start on another when Billy Applegate stopped beside me.

"Hey, Billy," I said.

"Hey, Delores."

I squinted across the playground at Elmer Tangiers and Dinky Nolan, who were tossing a baseball back and forth. Billy, Elmer, and Dinky were usually inseparable at recess. "How come you're not playing ball?" I asked him.

"Guess I'd rather talk to you." Billy's face went red. "Whatcha reading?"

I showed him the cover.

"*From the Mixed-up Files of Mrs. Basil E. Frankweiler,*" Billy read. "Ain't that the story about the two kids who run away then stay overnight in an art museum?"

A weak sneeze could've knocked me over. I never would've pegged Billy for a reader. But as Gramps once told me, *Two and two don't always add up to four when it comes to figuring out what makes folks tick.*

"Yep," I said. "That's the book."

"I'll have to read it when you're done." Billy stared at the ground. "Mind if I join you?"

"Be my guest."

Billy sat beside me. He rocked sideways, reaching into his pocket. Holding his hand out, he said, "Look what I got. It's a Matchbox car."

"I *know* it's a Matchbox car." I leaned in, inspecting the tiny frame. "It's also a Ford Thunderbird—1961, right?"

Billy's mouth dropped open. "How'd you know that?"

A small breeze whispered past. "I learned about cars from my grandpa," I answered.

Billy spun a tire on the Thunderbird. "He must be a good teacher."

"He was," I mumbled, so quietly Billy didn't hear.

"My oldest brother Ernie's the one who teaches me about cars. He works on an assembly line at the Ford plant, but he's saving up to have his own shop."

"How about you?" I asked Billy. "What do you want to do when you grow up?"

"Probably be a cop like my uncle Jim." He scratched his head. "You?"

I'd never given the notion much thought. "Maybe be a teacher or a librarian since I like words so much." I paused, adding, "I even keep a list of my favorite ones."

I was surprised how easily that last bit of information rolled off my tongue. I'd never told anybody about my Favorite Words list, not even Bailey. It wasn't that I'd decided not to tell her. My list was just something I'd always kept to myself—like what color underpants I had on. Some things you just don't advertise.

Billy closed one eye, squinting at me. "Can you tell me one of your words?"

I searched my brain for one that was extra-interesting. "Gabardine," I said.

Billy screwed his face up. "Sounds like the name of some snotty old rich lady."

I smiled. "You're right. A snotty old rich lady who wears too much perfume."

"And has a poodle with pink bows in its hair," Billy added. He faked a girl voice again. "Come here, poochie-woochie, Mommy Gabardine wants to take you for a ride in her Rolls-Royce."

We both laughed.

"Seriously," Billy said. "What's it mean?"

"Gabardine's a kind of cloth."

He nodded. "Try another one on me."

"Perdition."

Billy tugged his ear. "I ain't got the faintest idea."

"Perdition means something's in ruins. It's also another word for"—I whispered—"hell."

Billy grinned. "I got one for you now. My fourth-grade teacher Miss Magaldi used to use it all the time. Loquacious."

"Loquacious," I repeated. If words had a scent, loquacious would smell like wild roses—the kind that climbed our trellis back in Beaver Creek. "What's it mean?" I asked.

"Means you're a windbag and you talk too much."

"No way. It's too pretty. You could insult somebody without them knowing it."

"Yep. The first time Miss Magaldi used it on Anna Marie Armstrong, Anna Marie thanked her. She thought she was getting a compliment."

I smiled, adding *loquacious* to my list.

Perfect Score

The following morning there was still no sign of Wendy.

After our morning snack, Mrs. Meriwether gave me a special job for scoring 100 percent on our vocabulary test. I was the only person in the class to spell *obstinate* right and use it correctly in a sentence: *O.B.S.T.I.N.A.T.E. His mama told him to eat his broccoli, but he was <u>obstinate</u> and refused.*

For my reward, I got picked to take down our bulletin board. How doing extra work ever got to be a prize is beyond me. By the time I handed Mrs. Meriwether the stack of faded construction paper and swept the staples off the floor, my class had left for gym.

Mrs. Lovejoy's class—who had gym right before mine—had cleared out of the locker room. And I could hear my class through the wall, starting warm-up exercises. Quickly, I changed into my gym suit and sneakers. Starting toward the gymnasium, I heard a noise in the corner. Slowly, I moved toward the sound.

A girl wearing a shower cap and towel stood beside an open locker. Her back was to me as she hurried to step into her underpants. Grabbing her slip off a hook, she dropped the towel. A large bruise, dark as blackberry jam, covered one whole shoulder blade.

I drew in a sudden breath.

The girl turned.

"Wendy!" I gasped.

Wendy jerked her slip over her head, jabbing at the arm-hole till her hand poked through. She wrestled with her dress, then her tights. Finally, she reached inside her locker for her shoes.

"I—I didn't know you were in school today," I said.

"I missed my ride with my father and had to walk." Wendy talked fast, each word slamming into the next. "By the time I got here, gym class was half over. Mr. Hathaway made me do extra laps for being late, and everyone showered before me. I'm sure they're back in the room taking the social studies test. I'll probably get a zero for missing it. I need to get out of here. I have to find my"—she spun in a circle—"my shoes. Where are my damn *shoes?*"

I pointed to her hand.

"Oh," she said, dropping them both to the floor.

I thought of Lenny Potts Junior again. None of us—kids, lunch monitors, teachers—did anything at all to help him. I suddenly understood something: Doing nothing really is doing something. It's choosing to remain quiet when you know full well things aren't right.

Gramps's face flashed before me. *Speaking up takes courage.*

I couldn't do nothing again.

My bangs slipped loose from my barrette. Talking from

behind that hair curtain seemed to help me go on. "Wendy," I said, "how did you get your bruise?"

"I backed into a hook inside my closet. I told you how clumsy I am. Remember when I spilled juice on my tights?"

Of course I remembered. That was the same day I saw her welts. And there was no way she got those by being clumsy.

Wendy glanced at her Timex, motioning for me to move aside.

Instead I stepped in front of her. "Wendy, what really happened?"

"Dee-Dee, please, I'm in a hurry."

"Wendy, did someone . . . hit you?"

She exhaled loudly. "I *told* you. I fell on something in my closet."

"No, Wendy, you said you *backed into* something in your closet."

Wendy glared at me. Her gaze was a strong arm, holding me at a distance.

She kicked her locker door closed. The echo clattered through the large room.

Then Wendy pushed past me and was gone.

Part Three

Caught

In fourth grade, I had a rotten tooth pulled. I couldn't convince my tongue to stop probing the hole in my gum. Now I was doing something similar. Again and again, my thoughts returned to the gap in my heart left open by the sight of Wendy's bruise.

For the rest of the day, Wendy avoided me. When I stopped at her locker after school, she'd already gone. So I walked home alone.

Gram was still at work. She'd left me a snack on the kitchen table, but I didn't feel like eating. I changed out of my school clothes and into a sweatshirt and dungarees. Then I hopped in the backseat of the Bel Air and rolled my window down. I leaned forward, hugging Gramps's seat, pressing my face into the upholstery till my nose grabbed ahold of his smell. "Gramps," I said, "I'm in a bind. I know this girl named Wendy. She's funny and talented and smart, and I really like being her friend. There's a problem, though—I think somebody's hurting her. I tried talking with Wendy about it, but she clammed up." I sat back, curling my legs in. "What do you reckon I should do?"

Gram claims the Lord works in mysterious ways. That

we have to be on the lookout for signs. I watched Gramps's seat, like I half expected it might answer me.

A voice came out of nowhere. "Who ya talkin' to?"

I nearly leapt out of my skin.

Billy stood beside my window, his bike balanced between his legs.

Glaring at him, I said, "Haven't you ever heard of announcing yourself?"

"I did. I cleared my throat twice and said hi." His eyes wandered as he cased out the cab of Gramps's Chevy. "Who ya talkin' to?" he repeated.

I whipped the car door open. "That ain't any of your beeswax," I said. I stomped up our stairs, turning when I reached the top.

Billy let his bike drop. He started up the steps behind me. He held out a newspaper. "Here."

"Thanks," I said, waiting again for him to leave. The longer I waited, the more I realized I wasn't just plain mad about what he'd caught me doing. I was embarrassed, too.

Billy dragged his toe along our WELCOME mat. I suddenly wished it said GO AWAY!

"Sometimes I talk to myself, too," he said.

I folded my arms. "I wasn't talking to myself."

"But there wasn't anybody with you. Unless you stuffed 'em in the trunk."

Somehow that tickled my funny bone. I bit the insides of my cheeks to keep from smiling. "I've gotta start my homework," I said.

Billy didn't take the hint. "Is it true, what you were saying about Wendy?"

Again, I glared at him. "You were listening?"

"Not on purpose. I just happened to—"

"Stop!" I snapped. I parked my rump on the stoop. I needed time to think.

"I say you're on to something." Billy sat beside me. "You know, about somebody hurting Wendy."

"What makes you say that?" I asked.

"In third grade, me and Wendy had to sit together in art class. Miss Parr made us put our hands in this white chunky stuff that looked like barf and—"

"It's called *papier-mâché*."

"Well, Wendy spilled her bowl all down the front of her sweater. Miss Parr said she'd soak it for her. The dress she was wearing underneath had short sleeves. I noticed these bruises on her arms. Little round ones about the size of blueberries, all lined up in a row, as if"—Billy shaped his hands like claws—"somebody'd grabbed her real hard.

"There was another time, too," Billy said, "right after I got my job. I stopped to see if the Parishes wanted their paper delivered. Wendy's mother answered the door, acting like she was guarding Fort Knox. Wendy came into the room behind her, half asleep—she'd been out of school that day. When Mrs. Parish saw her, she ordered Wendy back to bed, but not before I got a good look at her face." He touched his eye, grimacing. "Wendy had a shiner like you wouldn't believe." Billy glanced my way. "You seen things too, haven't you?"

I wondered if I'd be betraying Wendy by answering him. Wendy might get mad if she knew we were talking about her. She might stop being my friend.

But I reminded myself: Doing nothing really *is* doing something. So I told Billy everything I'd seen. After I finished I said, "Whaddaya think we should do?"

"I have no idea." Billy fiddled with his shoelace. "My mama used to say one of the hardest things to learn is when to *speak up* and when to *shut up*. I guess I finally know what she meant."

A pain fluttered through me and I sat forward, hugging myself. I knew I couldn't say what I was thinking, that I was jealous he had a mama to give him advice, so I thought of something civil instead. "She sounds like a smart woman," I told him.

"Yeah," Billy said, "she was."

"Was?"

"She died." He tapped his chest. "Weak heart."

"Oh, Billy," I said, "I'm sorry."

Billy squinted into the sun. "I saved a bottle of her perfume. Sometimes I spray it in my room. My brother Clive says it makes me smell like a girl, but I don't care." He shrugged. "Girls ain't all that bad."

Tit for tat, Gramps used to say—meaning if a person gives you something, it's only fair you repay them. And Billy had given me his trust. Now it was my turn. "In the car earlier," I started, "I, um, I *was* talking to somebody. My grandpa. Except you couldn't see him 'cause he died. Three months ago."

"That's too bad," Billy said, looking like he understood. Then it hit me—he *did*.

Billy glanced toward the driveway. "Was that his car?"

I shook my head yes.

He stared at the SOLD sign. "Why's your grandma getting rid of it?"

"Gramps was the only one who drove."

"That stinks." Billy paused. "You're gonna miss that car, ain't you?"

My throat tightened. "More than anybody knows," I half said, half croaked.

Billy leaned to the side, reaching deep in the pocket of his trousers. When he drew his hand out, he was holding something—a brand-new Matchbox car. A Chevy Bel Air convertible, to be exact. "I bought this yesterday, 'cause it made me think of you." Billy's face went red. Honestly, I'd never known anybody who blushed as much as he did. "It's like your grandpa's," he said, "except for being red and white instead of turquoise and white, but the year's the same, 1957." He held his hand forward. "I want you to have it."

"Really?"

Billy nodded. He set the car in my palm.

"Well . . . thanks," I said.

Billy retied his sneakers and stood, adjusting his canvas bag. I noticed there were still several papers inside. "I better get going," he told me, "or crabby Mrs. Templeton'll be waiting with a royal piss-face."

He lifted his bike and hopped on, waving as he pedaled off.

I waved, too, surprised by what I was wishing: that Billy could've sat a spell longer.

Banana-licious Evidence

After finishing my Saturday cleaning jobs, I stood at the window, watching a cardinal crack seeds at Cousin Effie's feeder. I felt sorry for that little guy. I had a new winter coat to keep me warm. All that bird had was feathers.

The phone rang and Gram answered it. "Delores," she called, "it's Gwendolyn."

Wendy had barely said two words to me since I'd seen her bruise in the locker room. So when I heard her voice, sounding like nothing had happened, I nearly jumped out of my socks. "What are you doing?" I asked her.

"Not much," she answered. "I just finished the chore list my mother left me."

"Left you?" I twirled the curlicue cord around my finger.

"Her sister's birthday is today, and my mother's surprising her with a cake. She wanted me to go, too, but Aunt Claire's kids drive me crazy, so I begged her to let me stay home. I told her I wanted to practice my routine for the finals. She'd never say no to *that*. Anyway, Daddy gave me my allowance. I wondered if you'd like to see a movie."

"Sure," I said. "Are Anna Marie and Connie coming, too?"

"Well . . . I didn't ask them. I thought the two of us could go this time."

My smile stretched so far it could've snapped my face in two. "What time's the show?"

The balcony had a large CLOSED sign hanging from a red velvet rope. "Follow me," I whispered, sneaking underneath.

"But the sign," Wendy whispered, pointing.

I held the rope up for her. "*Closed* doesn't really mean closed. It means Don't-Get-Caught-'Cause-It-Isn't-Really-Open."

Wendy ducked under, clutching the popcorn she'd bought us.

We picked two seats in the first row. Over the balcony railing I recognized Billy Applegate's red head, parked beside Elmer Tangiers's shaved one. Elmer had his finger up his nose so far you'd think he was digging for gold.

The lights flickered and the satin curtain parted. The picture crackled and snapped, working to catch up with the sound.

Wendy and I sat back, the popcorn tub balanced between us.

I glanced down at Billy again. His elbow was bent on the

armrest and his chin was propped on his hand. He looked like he was thinking hard about something.

"Who are you staring at?" Wendy asked me.

"Nobody," I answered, jerking my head toward the movie screen.

The lights dimmed, just in time.

After the matinee we ambled through downtown Lakeville. Wendy paused in front of the ice-cream parlor. "Let's share a banana split, my treat."

Immediately, I thought of Wendy's diet. "But we already had popcorn at the movies—"

"Popcorn *without* added butter," Wendy corrected me. "Every calorie of which we burned off walking here. Besides, bananas are a fruit. And fruit is good for you." She held the door open. "Come on, Dee-Dee, I've lost ten pounds on my mother's diet. Don't I deserve a little reward?"

I shrugged. "Okay, if you say so."

We picked a table near the window. I dipped my spoon into that banana-licious concoction again and again, feeling as stuffed as one of Wendy's dogs. Finally, a lone maraschino cherry sat in the middle of the serving dish. Wendy popped it in her mouth, shot me a glance, and stood suddenly. "Do you remember how to do the Mashed Potato?" she asked.

How could I forget? Nearly everybody was doing the Mashed Potato at Opal and Ed Purdy's daughter's wedding two years ago. But if I even thought of dancing, I'd upchuck mashed *bananas*. "Sorry," I lied, "it's slipped my mind."

"How about the Twist, then?" Wendy sucked whipped cream off her thumb. "You must remember that."

I held my stomach. "Wendy, I don't—"

"That's okay, I'll show you." She grabbed my hands, yanking me upright. "Here's how Chubby Checker did it. First, put your arms out in front of you." Wendy demonstrated.

I didn't have much choice in the matter. I checked to make sure no one was looking. When I saw the coast was clear, I copied her.

"Good." She continued, "Now move your arms like you're holding a giant tray of cookies, offering them back and forth to the people on your left and on your right. Use your waist to turn. Left, right, nice and smooth. You don't want to spill your cookies."

I took a deep breath. "I'm trying not to spill my cookies, all right."

"Next, grind your toe on the floor. Pretend you're putting out a cigarette."

I moved my foot the way Wendy did. I had a cramp in my side that wouldn't stop.

Wendy danced beside me. "You're doing great!" she said.

Suddenly, music shot on. The soda jerk held up a radio, bobbing his head.

I closed my eyes, imagining nobody could see me. And something downright peculiar happened. The music tunneled underneath my skin. It traveled up my spine, then back down again. My belly stopped aching. Soon I was twisting my heart out, each back-and-forth turn sending little surges clean through me.

Wendy patted my arm. "Dee-Dee?"

I waved her hand away. "Not now."

"Dee-Dee," she shouted over the music, "it's important!"

I opened one eye. The music kept playing, but the spell was broken.

I followed the path of Wendy's gaze.

Across the street a blond-haired woman stepped out of a shiny red Firebird, closing the car door hard. Then she started down the sidewalk. There was no mistaking her limp. "Isn't that—"

"Yep." Wendy grabbed my hand. "And if she sees me in here, I'm in big trouble!"

War

We hurried down the street and turned the corner, cutting across the Woolworth's parking lot. We ducked behind the soda machine and dropped into a squatting position. Slowly, I stood, peering around the corner. Mrs. Parish was at the far end of the lot, her shadow slicing the macadam.

"Shoot!" I said. "She's headed straight this—"

The squeal of bike brakes interrupted me. I looked up, startled.

"What a stupid movie," Elmer Tangiers said. "Whoever heard of talking monkeys?"

"They weren't monkeys," Billy Applegate said back. "They were apes. Don't you know the difference?"

Elmer shrugged, digging in his pocket. When his hand came up empty, he swatted his handlebars, yelled, "Dang!" and pedaled off.

Billy was about to follow him when he noticed Wendy and me crouched beside the soda machine. "Hey," he said, smiling. "Whatcha doing down there?"

"Hiding from someone." I glanced toward Mrs. Parish hoping he'd catch my drift.

His eyes came to rest on Wendy's mother, whose gimpy gait wasn't slowing her pace one bit. "Yikes," Billy mumbled, gulping hard. When he crouched beside us, his knee clunked against mine. Blushing, he said, "I know it's none of my business, but this ain't the world's best hiding place. If somebody's coming from over there"—he pointed—"they can't see you. But if they're over there"—he tipped his chin toward the opposite end of the lot, the side Mrs. Parish would soon cross—"you're in plain sight."

"What do you suggest we do?" Wendy snapped.

"Find a better hiding place," he said, offering his hand to help us stand.

We must've followed Billy for a mile, at least. Finally, as

we cut across a scruffy field into a large wooded area, he said, "Almost there!" Twigs snapped beneath our feet. A flock of wild geese flew overhead. Billy stopped at the foot of a rickety-looking tree house. Waving his hand, he said, "Welcome to Fort Applegate!"

Billy climbed the ladder first, then Wendy, then me. The walls were made of plywood, and the roof had two plum-sized holes. An old brown rug covered the floor.

Wendy ducked to avoid a nail poking through the ceiling.

"Have a seat." Billy motioned toward a plaid sleeping bag crumpled in one corner. The fabric was covered with dog hair. Wendy and I sat on it anyway.

My cheeks tingled from the cold. My socks were soaked from plodding through the damp leaves. I hugged my knees, hoping to warm up a bit.

Billy dropped to the floor, and the fort shook. Wendy drew in a quick breath.

"Don't worry," he told her. "It's solid. My uncle Leo helped me build it two summers ago. 'Cept Uncle Leo's got a Texas accent so he calls it *Faarrrrrt Applegate.*"

Billy reached inside a cigar box and held out a handful of bubble gum. When I saw the brand name on the box— Topper Grandes—my heart went soft. They were the brand Gramps used to smoke.

We passed several minutes chomping away.

Billy glanced over at Wendy. "I'm, uh, sorry again about busting your thermos."

Wendy blew a giant bubble. She sucked it back against her lips with a loud crack. "That's okay," she said. "I have a new one now."

"Yeah," Billy said. "Delores told me."

Wendy looked from Billy to me. "Oh, really?"

Billy blushed again. "Yeah, we talk sometimes."

Wendy grinned. "I see."

Billy reached back inside the cigar box, removing a tattered deck of playing cards. "Feel like playing a game of War?" he asked us.

Wendy and I nodded.

Billy shuffled the deck. He turned up a ten of hearts in front of me, flipped over the queen of spades for Wendy, and dealt himself the eight of diamonds. He groaned.

Wendy reached for the cards, starting a pile beside her knee.

"So, Wendy," Billy said, "I think we lost the person who was trailing you."

Wendy squirmed on the sleeping bag. "For now, anyway."

Billy reached above his head. A Brooklyn Dodgers hat hung on a rusted nail. He shaped the cap around his fist, then plunked it on his head, tugging the rim into place. "I hope you ain't gonna have any trouble when—I mean *if*—the person catches up to you."

Judging by the look on Wendy's face, she was wondering the exact same thing.

Billy separated three more cards. He dealt himself the

five of clubs and me the seven of hearts. He turned up an ace in front of Wendy. "Hell's bells," he said to Wendy. "You're good at this game."

Wendy chewed her bottom lip. "You have no idea," she said, adding the cards to her collection.

Shelter

After church on Sunday our phone rang. Gram was frying peppers for scrambled eggs, and I was stretched out on the davenport reading a library book.

I was relieved to hear Wendy's voice on the other end. "What happened?" I rushed out. "Did you get in trouble for the banana split?"

"No." Wendy spoke softly. "My mother was downtown running errands for Aunt Claire. She didn't even see me."

"That's great," I said.

"Are you still coming over tomorrow?"

"I wouldn't miss it for the world."

The whole next day I watched the clock, waiting for school to end. Finally, the bell rang, and we were on our way.

As we turned down Wendy's street, I noticed her driveway was empty. "Where's your father's car?" I asked her.

"I have no idea," she said.

Inside, Wendy held up a small note left on the kitchen table. Out loud, she read,

> *Dear Pickle,*
> *I have to return to the office for some paperwork.*
> *Mrs. Jenkins is home if you need anything.*
>
> *Love, Daddy*

"Who's Mrs. Jenkins?" I asked her.

"Our next-door neighbor. She used to babysit me. My father adores her. My mother claims she's nosy." Wendy shrugged. "Just one of many things they can't agree on." Wendy opened the refrigerator and removed two Tab colas, flipping their tops with an opener. We clinked our bottles together, then sipped. I'd never tasted a diet soft drink before. I was surprised it wasn't half bad. "Follow me," Wendy said, opening a door onto a skinny, dark stairwell.

"Where are we going?" I asked.

"To the basement."

I'd only been in a basement once—beneath the Beaver Creek Grammar School during a tornado warning. I gripped the wooden railing, feeling with my feet for each step. The damp air tickled my nose. I sneezed. Once, twice, three times.

"Bless you, bless you, bless you," Wendy said.

"Thank you, thank you, thank you," I said back.

At the bottom of the stairs, Wendy clicked on a lamp.

An old plaid couch was parked against a concrete wall. Opposite that were three roll-out cots, a small refrigerator, and a table with mismatched chairs. "Does somebody live down here?" I asked her.

"Of course not. It's a fallout shelter, in case the Russians bomb us. Daddy said they'd probably target Cincinnati, since they have an air force base. But they could decide to bomb Cleveland, too, and that's a lot closer. Anyway, Daddy built this when I was in second grade. President Kennedy suggested it."

I stared at Wendy. "Your father knew President Kennedy?"

Wendy rolled her eyes. "President Kennedy said it on television. To everybody."

"Oh," I mumbled, embarrassed.

"Come on, I'll show you our gadgets." Wendy pointed to a huge white drum. "This is our portable latrine." She removed the round seat, peering through the center. She whirled around, patting a large square can. "And fourteen pounds of survival biscuits. And lastly"—she held up what looked like a fountain pen—"a radiation meter to measure the gamma rays in the fallout, so we know when it's safe to leave."

Wendy drew a curtain revealing shelves lined with everything from tuna fish to Tang. "This is our emergency food supply," she explained. "And this"—she reached behind the SPAM for a tall blue box—"is what we'll have to wear for our monthlies."

"Holy moly." I studied the pad she handed me. "Feels more like a mattress to me."

Wendy smiled. "Connie thought so too. In first grade a whole bunch of her mother's pads turned up missing. She found them, ten of them, in Connie's dollhouse."

"What were they doing in there?"

"Connie's Barbie dolls were having a slumber party. They were stretched out, comfortable as can be, sleeping on them!"

We both laughed.

The door at the top of the stairs shot open, scaring the bejeezus out of me.

"Hi, Daddy!" Wendy called.

But the voice that answered back wasn't his.

Trapped

"Gwendolyn," Wendy's mother called, "what are you doing in the basement?"

Wendy stiffened. "I, um, thought I heard a noise. It must have been a mouse."

She motioned for me to hide. I slipped behind the couch, crouching among the dust bunnies. My eyes itched and my nose prickled, and I prayed I wouldn't sneeze again.

Wendy walked to the bottom of the stairs. "I thought you had a hair appointment."

"I did," Mrs. Parish answered. "But Trudy left early with a headache, and that new Esther person couldn't keep up. I warned Trudy not to hire someone that *old*."

My face burned. I wanted to holler, *That person you're bad-mouthing is my grandma. And her name is Eunice, not Esther!*

"I rescheduled my appointment and picked up a few groceries instead," her mother continued. "I bought you something at the boutique next to the supermarket. Come upstairs and see what it is."

"I'll be right there," Wendy said. She rushed to my side, whispering, "My mother doesn't allow me to have friends in when no one's home. And the shelter is off-limits for visiting. If she finds you down here, I'll never hear the end of it."

"What should I do?" I whispered back.

"Wait here. I'll find a way to distract her. Sneak out the way you came in."

"Okay." I nodded.

"Gwendolyn," her mother called. "What's taking you so long? I'm excited to show you your gift. Hurry now. And don't forget to shut off the light."

Wendy smoothed her dress. *Sorry*, she mouthed, flicking the lamp switch. At the top of the stairs, she closed the door. Feet padded back and forth above my head.

The dark basement gave me the heebie-jeebies. I crossed the room on my hands and knees. Quietly, I climbed the steps. Light squeezed through the keyhole in the door. I knelt in front of it, peering into the kitchen.

Mrs. Parish handed Wendy a small gift box. Slowly, Wendy lifted the lid, then held up a thin silver necklace. A sparkly blue pendant hung from the chain. Light glinted off the stone as Wendy turned it round and round. "Oh, Mother," she said, "it's beautiful."

"I'm glad you like it. It's a blue topaz. I thought it would go nicely with your costume for the state finals. Let's see how it fits you." She motioned for Wendy to turn around, which she did, lifting her hair away from her neck.

Mrs. Parish clasped the chain in place. She took several steps back, smiling and nodding. "Gwendolyn, you look positively radiant. Come here and give your mother a big hug."

Wendy crossed the room, resting her head on her mother's shoulder, wrapping both arms around her waist. A jealous ache churned in my middle, and I wondered if I'd ever get to hug *my* mama like that.

Mrs. Parish perched her chin on top of Wendy's head, gently stroking her curls. Then, speaking so softly I had to strain to hear her, she said, "Gwendolyn, I regret what happened last week. I was wrong to lose my temper. I was so tired when I got home from Trudy's and found the kitchen a mess that I . . ."

I have to admit, I lost track of what Mrs. Parish was saying because I had an emergency to deal with. Another sneeze tickled my face, threatening to have its say. I pinched my nose and covered my mouth. Still, it escaped, followed by a small, shrill squeak.

Mrs. Parish glanced toward the basement door. "What was that?" she asked.

Wendy straightened, panic spreading clean across her face. "It was probably the mouse I heard earlier."

Mrs. Parish shuddered. "Remind me to have your father set some traps," she said, releasing Wendy from their hug. She walked to the counter, reaching inside a brown paper bag. "Since you're here, why don't you help me unpack these groceries?"

Wendy didn't seem too happy with her mother's request. Still, she felt inside a second bag, removed several cans, and clutched them to her. I watched as she crossed the room and began stacking them carefully in the pantry.

Her mother opened the refrigerator, rummaging around. "That's funny. I was *certain* I had three sticks of butter and I'm only finding two. Gwendolyn, do you know anything about this?"

"No, Mother. Why?"

"Well, I don't mean to bring up the past, but you did use a stick last week and forget to mention it."

"Mother, I told you, I didn't use the butter, I set the stick on the stove, and it melted. It was an accident. Besides"— Wendy glanced at the basement door again—"I was already punished for that, remember?"

Mrs. Parish took Wendy's chin in one hand. "Are you being fresh with me?"

Wendy smiled. A tight, pretend smile. "Of course not, Mother."

"Good. Because it would be a genuine shame to ruin such a nice conversation. And you know how I hate disrespect."

Wendy turned, mumbling something under her breath.

"I missed that, Gwendolyn."

"I was talking to myself, Mother."

Mrs. Parish folded her arms. "I asked you what you said."

"I was wondering wh-where the steak sauce goes," Wendy stammered.

Mrs. Parish grabbed Wendy's arm, spinning her around. "Don't lie to me, young lady!"

"Okay," Wendy blurted out, "I said disrespect isn't all you hate. Sometimes I think you hate me, too."

"Don't be silly. I'm your mother. It's my job to watch over you, to make sure you don't live on candy and buttered popcorn. After all, we wouldn't want Minerva Stern to have to roll you onto the stage, now would we?"

Wendy backed away. "That was a mean thing to say."

"Oh, Gwendolyn, please. Every calorie I count, every trip I make to Cleveland, every competition I help prepare you for—*everything* I do is for you. You know that."

Wendy reached back inside the grocery bag, removing a jar of tomato sauce. She glared at the basement door, a long, unbroken stare so fiery I could feel the heat through the keyhole. "You're wrong, Mother. Everything you do is for *you*." Wendy's face was red, a match ready to strike. "Because if I don't look good, you don't look good."

I drew in a sudden breath as Mrs. Parish's hand cracked hard against Wendy's face.

Wendy stumbled backwards. The jar smashed to the floor, and the sauce exploded.

"You clumsy girl!" her mother yelled.

Wendy ran from the room. Her mother followed.

All I could see through the keyhole was an empty, sauce-spattered kitchen.

Slowly, I opened the door. I knew I was supposed to leave. But I couldn't. I inched my way down the hall toward Wendy's room.

I paused outside, pressing myself flat to the wall, listening.

"I'd like you to apologize," Mrs. Parish said. But Wendy was silent.

I crept close to the door frame, peeking gingerly into the room.

Her mother's back was to me. She was snapping a black leather belt against her calf. Wendy leaned into her bed, her stuffed dogs lined up behind her.

The belt quivered, snakelike. "*Apologize*," Mrs. Parish repeated.

"Why should I?" Wendy's fingers curled into fists. "You've already found an excuse to hit me. An apology isn't going to change that."

"Very well," her mother said. "Then you may close the door."

I backed against the wall and held my breath for fear Wendy would see me. But she must've already guessed I was there. Quickly, she ducked her head into the hall and whispered, "Leave! Now! And don't tell!"

Her eyes were so sad I could feel my spirit wilt. "But, Wendy—"

She closed the door.

The belt whistled and cracked. "Wendy," I whispered.

As each blow landed and Wendy stifled a sob, I breathed her name.

Finally, I pried myself free. And I did what she had told me to do. I left.

Outside, the sky had grown gray. Storm clouds lashed at the waning sun. And every step—each slap of my Keds on those pristine sidewalk squares—echoed like the hot crack of leather.

Fallout

I collapsed on our cold concrete steps and buried my head in my hands.

A clatter rose in the distance. I looked up.

Billy was speeding down the dirt road, his canvas bag flapping behind him. When he reached our driveway, he let his bike drop, ripped the bag off his shoulder, and bounded toward me, landing close to my feet. "I tried . . . calling you . . . ," he huffed.

I shivered. "Whaddaya mean?"

Billy doubled forward, panting. His red plaid jacket

made him look like a lumberjack. He caught his breath, then stood. "When I was delivering papers, I saw you leaving Wendy's house. You looked a fright. So I finished my route as quick as I could, figuring I'd come by and check." His eyes met mine. "You all right?"

My teeth chattered. "I'm not sure."

Billy sat beside me. He slipped off his jacket, laying it across my shoulders. The warmth closed in around me.

"Something happen at Wendy's?" he asked.

"Billy, I don't know what I'm supposed to do or say. I— I—" A hiccupy sob trembled in my throat. I swallowed hard, forcing it down.

"That's okay." He stretched his arm across my back, gently pulling me into his side.

I leaned my head on Billy's shoulder. And even though his shoulder was bony and my neck felt like it might break, I was strangely comfortable, somehow.

"Life isn't fair," I told Billy.

"It ain't life's fault," Billy said. "It's people who mess things up."

My hands shook as I set the table for supper.

Gram was at the stove, adding flour and milk to the pork chop drippings. "Did you and Wendy have a nice visit?" she asked, stirring.

"Yes, ma'am," I fibbed. A utensil slipped out of my hand, clanging to the floor.

"Man, woman, or child?" Gram asked.

I picked up the spoon. "Child."

"I was surprised to see you home before me," Gram said. "Something cut your visit short?" At times I swear Gram can see right through me.

"Just a scrap," I lied again.

Gram lowered the flame beneath the saucepan. "Who was scrapping?"

"Wendy and her mama."

Gram harrumphed. "Can't say as I'm surprised. Mrs. Parish was mad as a wet hen about having to change her appointment after Trudy took sick. You'd think she had a date with Cary Grant the way she was carrying on." Gram turned, studying me. "Are you okay?" she asked.

"Yes, ma'am," I mumbled.

Tuesday and Wednesday crawled past. There was no sign of Wendy.

On Thursday she appeared, lunchbox in hand, starting down the sixth-grade hallway. I followed her to her locker.

"Wendy," I said softly, "I couldn't stop thinking about what happened Monday. Then, when you were absent, I was worried. I—I—" The words caught in my throat.

Wendy looked over her shoulder, making sure no one was listening. "Dee-Dee, I appreciate your concern, but I'm not at liberty to discuss the matter." She reached in her pocket, removing a lacy-edged envelope.

"What's that?" I asked her.

"My excuse for being absent. I had an ear infection." She tugged her left lobe.

Speaking up takes courage, Gramps reminded me.

I leaned closer. "Wendy," I whispered, "I know what your mother did, and why you were absent." I glared at the envelope. "That excuse is a lie."

Her hands trembled as she hung up her coat. "Like I said"—she collected her books and closed her locker—"I appreciate your concern."

"Wendy—" I started.

But she spun on her heel, hurrying down the hall to her classroom.

The Unexpected

Wendy barely spoke to me all day. When I stopped at her locker after school, she'd already left. So I waved good-bye to Anna Marie and Connie, and as they pedaled off, I started on my way, too, across the playground, down Main Street.

As if she'd dropped from the sky, Wendy appeared, falling into step beside me. "My birthday's November third," she reported matter-of-factly, "a week from Sunday. If I expect to get a gift from you, I suppose I'll have to be more pleasant." She smiled.

Being friends with Wendy was beginning to have more ups and downs than a roller coaster. But I was so relieved to hear her voice, she could've told me rats had built a nest in my lunchbox and I'd have jumped for joy. "No school on your birthday? Lucky stiff."

"I'd rather be in school," she answered. A sadness clung to her words. She waved her hand, as if to whisk it away. "When's your birthday?" she asked me.

"May fifteenth."

"That means"—she counted on her fingers—"I'll be twelve for six months before you catch up." She lifted her chin, gloating.

Wendy slowed to a stop, leaning against the concrete planter in front of the barber shop. Shriveled marigolds crowded its brown brittle soil.

I leaned beside her. "What are you doing for your birthday?"

"My mother makes those decisions," she said, snapping a dead marigold off its stem. Crushing the dried-up blossom into her palm, she changed the subject. "Earlier, at my locker . . . I'm sorry if I hurt your feelings. I didn't mean to. It's just that, well, I'm confused about a lot right now."

"Don't worry about it," I told her.

For several moments, we were quiet.

"So," I said, "do you want to get together again next Monday? Maybe you can come to my place instead."

"I'd like that," Wendy said, clapping the marigold seeds from her hands. "I'll ask my father tonight."

On Saturday morning, Gram and I cleaned the trailer, top to bottom. Then, after lunch, I used what I'd saved from my allowances to buy eight new picture frames at Woolworth's—six for Bailey's drawings and two for the paint-by-number dogs I'd made in fifth grade. I was never fond of painting—or coloring inside the lines—but Gramps had given me that set so I'd made it my business to finish the job.

While I was hammering and hanging, Gram moseyed past. Taking a gander, she asked, "Fixing up your room for Wendy's visit?"

"Yeah," I said. "I guess."

As I stood to put the toolbox away, a knock came at our door. "This wouldn't fit in your mailbox," the postman said, handing me a long cardboard tube. My name was printed on the label, and the return address was Bailey's.

"Thank you!" I said, rushing to peel the tape from the ends.

I opened the package and gasped. At the top of a large poster-sized paper, in fancy old-fashioned letters, Bailey'd written *Beaver Creek*. And below, in perfect detail, she'd drawn a map of the town. I traced my finger up and down each street, locating the library, the diner, the grammar school, the feed store, the bowling alley, the swamp. Eventually, I found our old house. I touched the driveway. Gram's climbing tea rose. The tree my Thinking Swing hung from.

My eyes filled. I drew a breath to stave off tears. Slowly,

I unfolded her letter, which was written on the backside of a shopping list.

> *Dear Delores,* she wrote.
> *I hope you like the map. It took me fifteen hours, so you better!*
> *Sorry I haven't written in so long. I hardly have any time to myself. Mama began having strange pains, and her doctor ordered complete bed rest, so I am doing all the cooking and cleaning. I'm plumb tuckered out before I even get my brothers and sisters off to school. And soon we'll be adding two more to the roost! Be glad you're an only child.*
> *Well, Little Joe is bugging me to read him a bedtime story. If he picks* The Three Little Pigs *again I'll scream! Bye for now.*
>
> > *Your friend,*
> > *Bailey*

I was tickled pink with Bailey's letter. But before I could kick up my heels and holler "hurray!" I turned the small paper over. Below the final grocery item, peanut butter, Bailey'd squeezed in a tiny PS:

> *Miss Kittle is starting a school newspaper. I signed up to do the artwork, Mary Stingpratt is going to answer etiquette questions, and Becky*

Montgomery plans to write a fashion column.
Isn't that exciting?

"Just ducky," I mumbled, and taped Bailey's map to my wall.

Later that evening, just after I'd gone to bed, the phone rang. Through the wall I could heard Gram talking in a low, muffled voice. After she hung up, she poked her head inside my room. "You asleep?" she asked softly.

I shook my head no.

Gram leaned against my bureau. "That was Mr. Maxwell," she said. "He's back from his business trip, and he'd like to come by within the week to pick up the Bel Air. He promised he'd call first. Anyway, I thought you'd wanna know. . . ."

I rolled over, hugging my pillow extra hard.

"I'm very sorry," Gram said, walking away, closing the door behind her.

"Not nearly as sorry as I am," I whispered to myself.

Tête-à-Tête Over Tab

After school on Monday, Wendy and I hurried down Main Street. A cold wind nipped at my fingers. Our breath froze in the air.

Halloween was only three days away. Plastic bats dangled from fake cobwebs outside Kemp's Hardware. A plug-in jack-o'-lantern glowed in the window of the record store. "Are you dressing up for Halloween?" Wendy asked me.

Bailey and I used to trick-or-treat every year—usually we planned our costumes together. But now Halloween didn't appeal to me. "I think I'm getting kind of old for it."

Wendy nodded, agreeing. She glanced at her mother's Firebird, which was parked in front of the Cut-n-Curl. "Before we go to your place, um, there's something I need to tell you." She motioned toward the soda shop.

My stomach did a nervous flip-flop. I followed Wendy inside. She ordered two Tabs and we sat at the counter, sipping away.

"Last Monday, at my house," Wendy started, "I know you were listening through the basement door. After I'd told you to wait downstairs—"

"I—I can explain," I blurted out, nearly choking on my soda.

"No. Let me finish."

A noisy radiator sputtered and hissed in the corner. I sat back, scared of what Wendy would say, afraid it might mark the end of our friendship.

"At first I didn't know you were there," Wendy said. "I was helping my mother unpack groceries, trying to prevent her from, well, exploding. But then I heard this noise behind the door."

"I sneezed," I admitted, embarrassed.

"When I realized you were there, I was horrified." Wendy shuddered. "I saw myself through your eyes—this pathetic girl who—"

"But I didn't think that about you!"

Wendy turned, ignoring me. "I hated you for being there." She jabbed her straw up and down in the soda bottle. "I knew I had to do something, to show you what I was capable of. To show myself. So I did something I've never done before. I told my mother what I thought, not what she wanted me to think. I talked back to her, Dee-Dee."

"But, Wendy," I whispered, confused, "you got a beating for that."

"Don't you get it, Dee-Dee? She would've hit me either way." Wendy reached across the counter, resting her hand on mine. "For the first time ever, I stood up to my mother."

Gram's Promise

The air smelled spicy, and I could tell that someone had been baking.

Wendy stopped on the gravel drive. "So, you really do live in a trailer."

"I prefer to call it a mobile home," I said. "Who told you?"

"Anna Marie. You know she can say mean things sometimes."

"Like what?"

"That girls who live in trailer parks never finish high school because they start having babies at fifteen. And all they eat is pork and beans, straight out of the can."

My cheeks burned. "What did you tell her?"

"I told her she shouldn't judge people by where they live." Wendy glanced at the Bel Air, giving it a good once-over. "This looks like the dream car you told us about."

I nodded. "Yep. A 1957 Chevy Bel Air convertible. My gramps's car."

Wendy touched the fender, drawing a line in the dust. "Why's your grandma selling it?"

"Gram doesn't have a license."

Wendy followed me up the steps. Inside, we set our

lunchboxes on the counter. "I can't believe you've got a washer and dryer," Wendy said. "We used to have a laundry room, before my dad built the shelter. Now we use a laundry service."

Gram scuffed toward us in her slippers. Trudy had changed her schedule so Gram would be home for Wendy's visit. "Hello, Gwendolyn. How's life treating you?"

Wendy smiled up at her. "Fine, thank you, Mrs. Colchester."

Gram reached into the cupboard, setting out two small plates. "I baked a blueberry pie. I'll cut you both a slice. Fetch the forks for me, Itch."

"Itch?" Wendy repeated.

I threw Gram an I-Can't-Believe-You-Said-That look.

"Oh, Lord!" Gram said, swatting at something invisible. "Did you see that?"

"See what?" Wendy said.

"That mosquito." Gram scratched her elbow, then slapped her knee. "He's been following me around all day, making me *itch* myself silly."

Gram sectioned off two pieces. My mouth was watering, so my brain took its time catching up. Recalling Wendy's diet, I whispered, "Should I say we don't want any?"

"No," she whispered back. "I don't want to hurt your grandma's feelings."

Wendy and I sat at the table. Gram placed a slice in front of each of us.

Wendy took a big bite, chewing. She dabbed her lips

with her napkin and told Gram, "That's the best blueberry pie I've ever tasted, Mrs. Colchester." She separated another bite, raising the fork to her lips. Except it didn't quite reach her mouth. The blue gooey mound slid off, landing smack-dab in the middle of Wendy's lap.

Gram patted her shoulder. "I was about to wash a load of coloreds. I'll scrub some lye soap on that stain and your dress'll be good as new. Stand up."

Wendy did. But when Gram stepped behind her, reaching to untie her bow, Wendy jerked away. "Wh-what are you doing?" she asked.

Gram drew back. "I'm sorry, Gwendolyn, I was only trying to—"

"I'll undress myself," Wendy said. "In the other room."

"Oh, mercy. Neither you nor Delores has got anything to hide." That was her way of saying we were both still flat as pancakes. "Stay where you are. I won't look. You got a slip on, don't you?"

Wendy nodded. She watched Gram return to the sink, shucking peas. Slowly, she lifted her dress. Every few seconds she stopped, tugging her slip into place. The fabric cleared her shoulder blades, then her neck. But on its way up and over her head, a button got stuck in her curls. "You're caught," I said. "I'll help."

"No!" Wendy pushed my hand away.

Gram turned, then gasped. Her colander dropped. Peas bounced across the floor.

The welts from Wendy's beating had faded, but they

were replaced by new bruises. Purple fist-sized bruises, visible around the edges of Wendy's slip.

Gram moved slowly toward her. "Child, what happened to your back?"

My eyes begged Wendy, *Tell her. Tell her!*

Wendy stumbled backwards, banging into Gram's maple hutch. The ceramic knickknacks wobbled. "I—I was bouncing on my pogo stick in the driveway, and—and I fell. Against the garage door. I'm so clumsy, I—"

Gram stepped forward again. "Those don't look like falling-down bruises to me."

"Well, they are!" Wendy stomped her feet. Gram's glass bunny toppled to the floor and smashed into tiny white shards.

Quickly, Wendy's arms flew in front of her face. She crossed them, as if she was protecting herself.

"Gwendolyn," Gram said softly, "put your hands down, child. Ain't nobody here gonna hurt you."

Slowly, Wendy lowered them. "Mrs. Colchester, I told you how I hurt my back. Now, please"—she blinked away tears—"stop asking me questions."

We were all silent. The refrigerator hummed in the corner.

"I've got an idea," Gram said finally. She removed her bust of Jesus from the hutch, staring deeply into His eyes. "You tell me who was beating on you, 'cause I got a real strong feeling that's how you got those bruises. And I'll promise you, with the Lord as my witness, that I will never tell the person who hurt you what I saw. Deal?"

Wendy hesitated. Her eyes danced from Gram to me, then back to Gram again. "No offense, Mrs. Colchester, but my family's not very religious. Would you mind doing the 'cross your heart and hope to die' thing for me?"

The word *die* made me wince. I prayed Gram knew what she was doing.

I watched as she drew an X across her bosom.

Wendy chewed her lip. "It was . . . my mother."

Gram sighed, touching Wendy's arm. Then she bent to collect the busted bunny.

School Night Sleepover

Gram never allowed Bailey and me to have sleepovers on a school night, but she made an exception for Wendy. Lucky for us, Mrs. Parish still wasn't home when Wendy called to ask permission. She begged her father for five minutes, but I could tell she wasn't getting anywhere. When Gram left the kitchen for a moment, Wendy crossed her fingers, whispering into the phone. "Daddy, I completely forgot that I have a social studies report due tomorrow on the state of Florida. I haven't even started it yet. If I get an F, Mother will be very upset. But if I stay here, Dee-Dee can help me—she used to live in Florida. *Please*, Daddy, can you think of something to tell Mother? Just this once."

Finally, after more hemming and hawing, Mr. Parish agreed.

As I set the table for supper, Wendy lifted a teaspoon, squinting into its silver curve. "What are you doing?" I asked her.

"We're always upside down," she said, handing me the spoon. "Look."

I studied my reflection. Sure enough, I was doing a head-stand.

Quickly Wendy flipped the handle in the opposite direction. "When I was little," she said, "I would do this over and over, hoping to catch myself upright."

Gram filled our milk glasses. "Supper's ready," she announced. "Time to wash your hands."

Wendy flipped her spoon one final time, then followed me to the sink.

Wendy liked my room. She paused before the sketches I'd framed. "I didn't know you were an artist."

"I'm not. My friend Bailey drew those."

Wendy studied the portrait of Miss Billings. "Who's Bailey?"

"She was my best friend in Beaver Creek. Since second grade."

"What's it like, having a best friend for that long?"

I stared at Bailey's picture of my Thinking Swing. "Like never having to explain much, 'cause the other person's got you figured out." I squinted at the swing's worn seat, the frayed rope. "Like feeling somebody's in your corner, no matter what."

"Wow." Wendy forced a smile. "Where do I sign up?"

"What do you mean?" I asked.

"I've never had a best friend." She looked away. "Did Bailey make the dog paintings, too?"

"No," I admitted, "they're from a paint-by-number set Gramps gave me."

She studied the dog with the white fur and black spots. "He looks like Bruce."

I squinted at his golden-brown eyes. "You're right," I agreed. "He does."

We spent the rest of the evening stretched out on my fuzzy throw rug, listening to my transistor radio. I loaned Wendy a pair of pajamas. Just before nine o'clock, we said our good-nights to Gram, and I folded my bed back for Wendy. She slipped below the blankets, tugging them up to her chin. "Your pillow smells nice," she said, hugging it.

I unrolled my sleeping bag on the floor beside her. "What's it smell like?"

She shrugged. "Like you, I guess."

In the morning we woke to the clang and clatter of Gram preparing breakfast.

"G'morning," she called, carrying a platter to the table. School-day breakfasts usually consisted of cereal and toast. Wendy was getting a pampering. "Hands clean?" she asked.

"Yes, ma'am," we answered, sitting down.

I bowed my head and said the blessing. Gram mumbled along. When I was finished, she stood, saying, "Oops, forgot the ketchup."

I handed Wendy the platter, which was mounded with eggs, sausage, and home fries.

"Scrambled eggs are my favorite," she said. "Except I never get to have them."

Gram returned from the fridge with the Heinz bottle. "Why's that?"

"My mother soft-boils my eggs. She says they have fewer calories."

Gram shook ketchup on her eggs. Then she passed the bottle to me.

Wendy studied us. "My father does that, too. Actually, he pours ketchup on almost everything. Last year on my father's birthday, the people at his office gave him a gag gift—an entire case of Heinz."

Gram laughed. "Where's your daddy work?" she asked.

"The Bradley Insurance Agency. Why?"

Gram stood, carrying the empty platter to the sink. "Just curious, is all."

The Fight

That next day I walked Wendy home after school, same as always. Pausing at the top of her street, I noticed two familiar cars in her driveway. "How come your dad's home?" I asked her.

"I'm not sure. His agency has their weekly sales meetings Tuesday afternoons." She bit her lip, looking worried. "Not much would drag him away from that."

Wendy had me worried, too. "Call me later," I said. "Even if everything's okay."

She nodded.

I headed home, moving as fast as my cold legs would carry me.

Gram was in the kitchen, a vegetable peeler in one hand, pacing. "I got a hankering for scalloped potatoes," she informed me.

"Why aren't you working?" I asked her.

"Trudy let me leave early." She looked away. "I had a delivery to make."

"What kind of delivery?"

She ignored my question. "How's Gwendolyn?"

"Okay, considering. Gram, what's wrong? Why are you pacing?"

Gram pulled out a chair and sat down. "I didn't sleep a wink last night, and I wasn't worth a curse at work today. I can't get that child's bruises out of my mind."

"I know what you mean," I agreed.

"How long have you known?" Gram asked.

"For sure, since last Monday. I overheard Mrs. Parish giving Wendy a whipping. But I've suspected something since the day Wendy's thermos got busted and she was scared about her mama finding out about it that I—" I stopped myself.

Gram eyed me sternly. "That by any chance the same day you came by Trudy's, begging me for the money for a lunchbox?"

I hung my head. "Yes, ma'am. I'm sorry for lying. I was only trying to protect Wendy. She made me promise to keep quiet, just like she made you promise not to tell anybody about the bruises you saw."

Gram stood, pointing the peeler at me. "You got that wrong. I gave Wendy my word that I'd never tell *the person who hurt her* what I saw." She walked to the pantry, removing several potatoes from the sack. "I never forget a promise."

Gram fell asleep watching television. It was past my bedtime, but I was way too jittery to sleep.

When the program ended, the phone rang. I leapt at it, answering before the second ring. "Wendy?" I blurted out. "Is that you?"

"Yes, Dee-Dee, it's me." Her voice sounded small.

A horn tooted. A siren wailed. "Where the heck are you?"

"I'm at a phone booth."

I pressed the receiver closer to my ear. "Where?"

Her teeth chattered. "The sign says Central Avenue, but—*oh!*—"

"What happened?" I gripped the phone.

"A man stumbled against the booth. He looked drunk. He's gone now."

"Wendy, where's Central Avenue?"

A second siren sounded. "Cleveland. A part I've never been in."

I glanced at the clock, confused. "But your dance lessons were over a long time ago. Did your mother's car break down or—"

"I didn't go to my dance lesson tonight. I missed it because my parents were fighting, worse than ever before. I tried to sleep, but my head was splitting from the noise. I grabbed my coat and some money and left. I started walking, but I got cold, so when I saw a bus I got on. I rode it to the end of the line."

"What were your parents fighting about?" I asked her.

"A letter my father got at work."

"Who was it from?" I asked.

"He doesn't know. It wasn't signed. And there wasn't a return address or a postmark. It must have been hand-delivered."

"What did the letter say?"

"That God sees everything and knows everything, and He knows something evil is happening under our roof."

I clenched the phone hard. "Wendy, we've gotta get you someplace safe. Can you take another bus back here?"

"No. They stopped running at ten."

My mind raced. I closed my eyes, hoping to quiet my thoughts. When I opened them, I was staring straight at the picture of Gramps that Gram keeps on the end table. His face had that I Double-Dog Dare You expression that could coax the stripes off a tiger. A chill rattled my bones. Gramps was trying to tell me something.

Stretching the phone cord, I reached inside the junk drawer, feeling around. "Is anything open?" I asked Wendy.

"There's a place across the street. Lucky's Burgers. The lights are still on."

"Good. Order a hot cocoa. Drink it slow so you'll have a place to wait for me."

"Wait for you? Dee-Dee, how are you planning to get here?"

My fingers touched what I was hunting for. "Leave that to me," I told her.

Sojourn

Gram's face was blue in the TV light. A soft snore rattled in her throat. "Gram," I said, shaking her shoulder, "Gram, come on, wake up."

"What's going on?" she grumbled.

"We have to go somewhere."

She squinted up at the clock. "Is this some kind of joke?"

"No, ma'am."

"What's that noise?" Gram bolted upright.

"I can explain."

She stomped to the door. Her hand flew to her chest. "Sweet Jesus! Who started your grandpa's Bel Air?"

"I did."

Gram whirled around. "Well, go turn it off!"

"Sorry, ma'am. I can't. We need that car."

There was fire in her eyes. "You aren't listening to me. I said—"

"Wendy ran away from home, Gram."

"She what?"

"She called from a pay phone in Cleveland. Her parents were having a terrible fight about a letter her father got."

Gram stopped dead.

"It said the Lord knows there are evil goings-on at Wendy's house," I continued, waiting for Gram's response.

"Give me a minute to change," she called, hurrying down the hall. When she reappeared, she was fully dressed, tying a scarf around her pin curls. She grabbed her winter coat and handed me mine. "We'll walk to the station and take the next bus out."

"The buses stopped running at ten."

She glanced toward the driveway. "Itch, I ain't been behind the wheel of a car since before I married your grandpa. I wouldn't know the first thing to do."

"I can show you, Gram." I took her arm, leading her gently toward the door. "I've seen Gramps drive a million times. And I tried it myself a time or two."

She glared at me. "He let you drive that car?"

"Only on the back roads."

Leaves covered the driveway, crunching beneath our feet. I held the door open, and Gram lowered herself into the driver's seat. The upholstery squeaked, exactly like it used to with Gramps.

"Okay," I said, hopping in the other side. "First, put your foot on the brake."

Gram hesitated. "If I get caught driving this car without a license, I—"

"Wendy's waiting."

"The brake," she repeated, flooring the wrong pedal. The car *varoom*ed and Gram jumped.

"That's the gas," I said calmly.

Gram pressed the second pedal. The engine purred. "What's next?" she asked.

"Take this"—I set her hand on the shift—"and slide it to D." When she did, the car jerked forward. "Now lift your foot off the brake. Press it on the gas, real gentle-like."

Gram tapped the pedal with her toe and we lunged ahead, gravel popping beneath us. Again and again, she tapped and released, till we'd hiccupped the length of our driveway and started up the dirt road beyond.

I dug through the glove compartment, searching for the map Leroy'd bought us at the gas station. I opened it across my lap and clicked on Gramps's emergency flashlight, searching till I found Central Avenue.

At the corner, Gram stopped, staring at the deserted intersection ahead.

I pointed to the turn signal. "That's your directional. We're going right."

Gram flipped the silver wand. *Pa-toink, pa-toink, pa-toink,* the signal sounded. Her thumbs did a nervous dance on the steering wheel.

"Gram?" I said softly.

"Dang car smells just like Orville," she said. A tear dribbled down her cheek. Then, smooth as can be, Gram lifted her foot off the brake pedal, rested it on the gas, and took off.

We found Lucky's Burgers and stopped at the curb. Actually, Gram drove partway onto the curb and then stopped, but I didn't say a word.

I spotted Wendy the second we walked through the door—sitting at a table, sipping from a large white mug. Her nightgown hung beneath her jacket, and she was wearing shoes but no socks. Her curls were limp. She looked positively *destitute*.

Wendy leapt up. She ran to me, hugging me hard. Turning to Gram, she said, "Mrs. Colchester, may I stay at your place tonight?"

"Of course you can, Gwendolyn. As soon as we tend to some business."

Wendy studied Gram's face. "What kind of business?"

Gram motioned toward the car, fishing the keys from her pocket. "You'll see."

Wendy paused beside the Bel Air. "Mrs. Colchester, um, I thought you didn't have your driver's license."

Gram opened the door and held the seat forward. "Your point being?"

Wendy shrugged her shoulders and ducked inside. "Nothing, ma'am."

Gram drove slowly, returning the same way we came. Back in Lakeville, she asked Wendy her address.

"But, Mrs. Colchester, you said I could—"

"I know what I said," Gram interrupted, "and I never go back on my word. Now, where do you live?"

"But if I'm staying with you tonight, then why do I have to—"

"Gwendolyn," Gram said, adjusting the rearview mirror,

staring down Wendy's reflection, "don't test an old lady's patience."

"Twenty-two Hawthorne Avenue," Wendy mumbled, slumping back in her seat.

Homecoming

Gram pulled in behind Mrs. Parish's Firebird. "Come with me, girls."

When she stepped out, the cold nipped at my knees. "Gram, it's almost midnight."

"Don't look like anybody's sleeping to me," Gram said. She was right. Every window was lit. When Wendy hesitated, Gram reached for her hand. "You ain't alone," she said. "We're a team. Three people who know your mama's been hurting you. Three people who wanna see it stop."

Gram started up the walk. Slowly, Wendy and I followed.

Gram rang the bell and Mr. Parish appeared, still dressed in his work suit and tie. "Pickle!" he said, drawing Wendy into his arms. "Where have you been? I've called everyone we know trying to find you. We were worried sick."

Gram cleared her throat. "I'm Eunice Colchester," she

told Wendy's daddy. "And you already know my grand-daughter, Delores."

He tugged his ear, perplexed. "Does this mean my daughter was with you?"

"I'd be happy to explain all that, Mr. Parish. But it's a tad chilly out here."

"Of course. I'm sorry." He held the door open. "Please, come in."

Gram collapsed on the long green sofa. I sat beside her, staring at the tall stone fireplace. Wendy's school pictures lined the shelf.

Mr. Parish started toward the kitchen. "I'll have my wife make us some coffee."

Wendy stiffened. "Don't wake her, Daddy. I can make it."

"Don't be silly, Pickle. How could your mother be sleeping at a time like this?"

Mrs. Parish appeared, knotting the belt on a long silky robe—a fancy robe like the ladies in Gram's soap operas wear. "Gwendolyn," she cooed, limping across the room. "Thank goodness, you're all right. Wherever have you—" She noticed Gram and stopped suddenly. "Why, you're the woman Trudy hired at the Cut-n-Curl. Esther."

"Eunice," Gram corrected her. "Eunice Colchester." She reached over, patting my shoulder. "And I believe you know my granddaughter, Delores."

She squinted, looking confused. "I haven't had the pleasure."

Gram shot me a curious look.

"I, um, visited on a Monday," I said, "when Mrs. Parish had a hair appointment."

Mrs. Parish stared at me. Then quickly she turned to face Wendy. "All that matters is that you're home." She reached to touch Wendy's cheek.

Wendy flinched.

Mrs. Parish took a small step back. "Gwendolyn, your father and I need to speak with Mrs. Colchester about what happened this evening. You and Delores can visit in your room. Come with me to the kitchen. I'll make you a warm drink to take along."

Wendy didn't budge. I crossed the room. "Let's go," I whispered in her ear.

"We need to stay with your grandma," she whispered back.

"Pickle," her father said, "it's not polite to whisper. Do as your mother says."

The tall dark clock beside the fireplace chimed. A tiny door opened. A miniature blue bird ducked his head out, calling "Cuckoo! Cuckoo! Cuckoo!" twelve times in all before the door closed and the bird disappeared.

"Mrs. Colchester," Wendy said, "could we please leave now? My stomach hurts."

"Wendy," her father said firmly, "Mrs. Colchester isn't in charge—*we* are. Go with your mother and get the drinks. Now." He gave her a nudge toward the kitchen.

Wendy whirled around, smacking his hand away. Hard.

Mr. Parish stood there, stunned.

"Do you finally understand what I mean, Dennis? That's a perfect example of what I deal with every day."

Wendy turned to her mother. "What *you* deal with every day?"

"Yes, Gwendolyn, that's what I said." Her mother started for the kitchen.

She didn't get far. Wendy dove at her. Grabbing her mother's arm, pulling on it, she screamed, "What *you* deal with every day? How about what *I* deal with every day?"

Mrs. Parish tried to pry Wendy off. "Dennis," she cried, "do something!"

Gram stood, barreling toward the center of the room. She held her arms out, blocking Wendy's father. "Listen to your daughter!" she told him.

I hurried to Gram's side, locking arms with her.

Everyone started hollering at once.

"Wendy, release your mother!"

"Mr. Parish, let Gwendolyn talk!"

"Dennis, get this child off me!"

"Gram, hold tight!"

Then one voice rose above the rest. Wendy's mother cried, "Damn it, Gwendolyn, you're hurting me!"

And that was when Wendy let go.

The Truth Comes Out

"I'm hurting *you*," Wendy spat. "Isn't *that* a switch!"

Mrs. Parish stood at attention. "Dennis, our guests have witnessed enough of our family scuffle. Why don't you see them to the door?"

He didn't. Instead he knelt in front of Wendy. Softly, he said, "What are you saying? Is someone hurting you? The letter I received—"

Mrs. Parish pushed between them. "Good heavens! Must we play another round of Guess What the Crazy Letter Means? Your brother probably sent it from the nuthouse!"

Mr. Parish's face reddened. "Leave Ray out of this, Millicent."

Gram ahemed. "Mr. Parish, I wrote that letter."

Wendy's mother's mouth dropped.

"But . . . *why?*" her father asked.

Gram faced Wendy. "Tell him, Gwendolyn."

Wendy bit her bottom lip. "I—I . . . can't."

"Then show him," I whispered. "I'll help you."

When Wendy turned, I slipped her coat off, thinking of the first day we'd met and how I'd fixed the catch in her zipper. I parted Wendy's curls. Several buttons lined the back of her flowered nightgown. I nudged the top one through its slot. Then the second.

Wendy's mother started toward us. "Gwendolyn, let's get some rest . . ."

"No," Wendy said. It stopped her mother in her tracks.

I undid the last button, pressing the fabric flaps open. Then I stepped away.

Her father drew in a sudden breath. He moved closer, gently touching Wendy's back. When she winced, his eyes filled. "My God, how did you get these bruises?"

Wendy hesitated. Then she lifted one arm, pointing a single finger at her mother.

Mrs. Parish gasped. "Dennis, she's lying!"

Wendy's father was silent for a long moment. Finally, he said, "Wendy, this is a very serious accusation you're making. . . ."

Mr. Parish kept talking, but I stopped listening. I was too busy watching Wendy—folding into herself, growing smaller and smaller with each breath.

I was shaking. Head to toe.

Speaking up takes courage, Gramps reminded me.

I know that, Gramps. But—but—

No, you don't know, Itch. 'Cause you ain't been put to the test. Not when the stakes are high. You wanna be like me? This is your chance, kiddo.

My forehead was clammy. I swallowed hard. "Wendy's not lying!" I blurted out.

"Oh, come now," Mrs. Parish said. "Why on earth would my husband take your word on—"

"Listen!" Gram interrupted. "The Lord don't judge us by our social standing, if that's what you're suggesting. He judges us by how we carry on with others"—she waved her hand in Wendy's direction—"and whether we do right by our kin. Now, let my granddaughter speak her piece."

Mrs. Parish folded her arms.

The room was so quiet I could hear the cuckoo clock tick.

All eyes were on me.

I opened my mouth. "I . . . I . . . ," I started, but a rasp was all that escaped.

"Mrs. Colchester, your granddaughter has no idea what goes on in this house," Mrs. Parish said.

Come on, Itch. You can do it.

I forced the words out. "I know plenty!"

Mrs. Parish's stare scalded me. "Pardon me?"

My heart hammered in my chest. "Last Monday, when you got home, I . . . I was here. Wendy, she—she told me to hide. . . .

"When you and Wendy were unpacking groceries, you—you got mad at her. For talking back. You had a black belt you tapped against your leg. You told Wendy to apologize. But she wouldn't. So—so—you—"

Whistle, crack!

"—you hit her. Again and again and again . . ."

Suddenly I was bawling my eyes out.

I didn't care who saw.

Those tears were right at home, cooling my fiery cheeks.

Nocturne

I'd never seen a man cry before. Gramps almost did, once—the day he got the phone call from Sarasota about his sister Winnifred's passing. His eyes got glassy and red, and I expected him to reach for a handkerchief. Instead he reached for his car keys and went for a very long drive. But Mr. Parish handled sadness differently—he dropped down in his recliner, landing hard as a sack of cement, and cried his heart out.

Gram suggested Wendy spend the night with us. Mr. Parish agreed.

A single streetlamp glowed at the bottom of our road.

An owl perched on a crooked branch, calling *hooooo, hooooo, hooooo.*

Gram warmed milk to help us sleep. She paused in the doorway to my room as Wendy unpacked her suitcase. "You were brave tonight, girls. Either of you need anything before I settle down?"

Now, Gram's not the type folks usually cozy up to. So as I watched Wendy rush over, wrapping both arms around her thick middle, I was just as surprised as Gram was. She lifted her hands—slowly, like she was trying to figure out what to do with them. They came to rest on Wendy's head. "You hug like my daughter, Ruby Lee, used to," she said, smoothing Wendy's hair. "Like you mean business."

Gram turned to leave, her slippers scuffing toward her room.

Wendy burrowed beneath the blankets, tucking Bruce in beside her.

I slid into my sleeping bag. Several minutes later I whispered, "You asleep?"

"Wide awake. I keep seeing my father crying. Do you think he's upset with me?"

"No, why would he be? Your mother's the one who did something wrong."

"But maybe she acts the way she does *because* of me," Wendy said.

"What do you mean?"

"When I was young—before I started taking dance lessons—we colored pictures together, and she braided my hair and made me tuna melts. She almost never hit me. But as I got older, she seemed . . . angrier." Wendy fiddled with Bruce's ear. "What if I'm the one who changed? What if I became someone she couldn't love anymore?"

Her words hung there, like a helium balloon that couldn't get past the ceiling.

I raised up on one elbow. "I used to think it was my fault that my mama ran off. One day I asked Gramps, 'What was wrong with me, anyway? Was I colicky? Did I fuss too much? Was I ugly?'"

"What did he say?" Wendy asked.

"He told me I was the most perfect baby he'd ever laid eyes on, and Mama's leaving had nothing to do with me and everything to do with her. He also said being born female doesn't guarantee somebody's got the knack to be a good mama."

"He said that about his own daughter?"

"Gramps didn't mince words."

"If your grandpa were here, what do you think he would say about my mother?"

"I reckon he'd say, *If Itch's mama's missing her knack, could be Wendy's mama is, too.*" My face flushed when I realized I'd called myself Itch.

"What was your grandpa like?" Wendy asked.

I thought of the picture of him on my dresser, assembling the bike he bought me for my sixth birthday. Parts were strewn across the floor—a kickstand here, a training wheel and a handlebar there. Gramps had every tool out of his case, trying to fit those parts together. "What was he like?" I repeated. "Gramps made all the pieces connect."

Wendy rolled over, gathering the covers around her. Eventually, she drifted off.

Not me. My thoughts were bouncing back and forth, flashing and pinging, refusing to let me sleep. I tiptoed across my room, slid my feet inside my shoes, grabbed my coat and gloves, and stepped outside.

The moon balanced on the tip of a distant pine, dabbing light on the blue-gray landscape. The colors reminded me of a painting Bailey'd shown me in a library book—*Nocturne*, which means night, but sounds a whole lot prettier. And a whole lot more serious, too. Like a night that could change you. A night that could "move mountains," as Brother Thompson used to say.

I crossed the field I'd walked through with Billy to go fishing. Where wildflowers once sprouted and lightning bugs had blinked on and off, scraggly stalks poked through the cold earth. I spotted a tree stump and sat down.

Staring up at the stars, I whispered, "Gramps, I know you were there, at Wendy's. You were watching me, helping me stay strong, weren't you?" I focused on the brightest star, which burned even brighter for several seconds, and I suddenly understood something. The people we care about don't just live outside us and when they're gone, they're gone. They live inside us, too. In our hearts and in our thoughts and in a thousand invisible pockets we don't even realize we own. Gramps would always be with me.

But he would be there in a new way. A quiet way.

Halloween

When my alarm clock rang, I groaned. I'd barely slept forty winks. Wendy looked as tired as I felt. We changed into our school clothes and started toward the kitchen.

"G'morning," Gram called, carrying pancakes and eggs to the table. "Your daddy phoned, Gwendolyn. He said not to wake you. He wanted to know how you're doing."

Wendy's face twisted. "How did he sound, Mrs. Colchester?"

"Worried about you, mostly." Gram motioned for us to sit. "Your mother and him talked most of the night. She finally admitted she's been hurting you. Your father'll be there when you get home from school. He plans to drive you to your dance class."

Wendy swallowed hard. "Did my mother . . . go somewhere?"

Gram nodded. "To your aunt's house. She's gonna stay there till they figure out what to do next."

"Oh." Wendy unfolded her napkin. She stared down at her lap.

I said grace and passed the platter. We ate quietly, barely speaking.

Afterwards, Gram handed us our matching lunchboxes, filled with our matching lunches.

Starting up our road, kicking a stone, Wendy said, "Life stinks," and for once, she sounded like a kid.

"It isn't life's fault," I said, quoting Billy. "It's people who mess things up."

By lunch Wendy and I acted like zombies. Anna Marie and Connie were too busy discussing their Halloween plans to notice.

Later, walking home, the cold seemed to help perk us up.

"Smells like snow," Wendy said, sniffing the gray air.

"Snow has a smell?" I asked.

She nodded. "Haven't you ever noticed?"

"I lived in Florida, remember? I don't even know what it *looks* like."

"I love snow," Wendy said. "Every year, I pray for a blizzard on my birthday."

With everything that had happened, I'd lost track of Wendy's birthday. I remembered what she'd told me—about her mother being in charge of all the planning. "I've got an idea," I said. "What if I ask Gram to have your party at our place? She likes baking—she'll probably offer to make you a cake."

Wendy smiled. "Really?"

"I'll check with her tonight."

⌧　⌧　⌧

Gram liked my idea just fine. Within minutes, she'd hauled out her baking file and spread cake recipes from one end of the counter to the other.

After supper, while she relaxed on the davenport watching *Daniel Boone*, I sat at the kitchen table, reading. Considering where we lived, I didn't expect much traffic for Halloween. So I was pleasantly surprised when a knock came and I opened our door to find three boys yelling "Trick or treat!"

Our front light fanned across the driveway. I held out the tray of candied apples Gram had made.

The robot and the mummy grabbed one, dropped it into their pillowcase, and skedaddled next door to Cousin Effie's. But the skeleton just stood there.

I glanced down at his holey sneakers. "Billy?"

He lifted his mask, propping it on top of his head. "Hey, how'd you know?"

"Lucky guess."

"How come you're not trick-or-treating?"

I shrugged. "Not in the mood, I s'pose."

"Delores!" Gram hollered. "You're letting a draft in!"

"Sorry!" I called. I grabbed my jacket and stepped outside, pulling the door closed behind me. I sat on a step and Billy sat beside me, tipping his pillowcase toward me.

"Thanks," I said, unwrapping a peppermint pattie.

Billy opened a Mallo Cup, and we chewed our candy in silence.

When we were finished, he said, "At school today, I, um,

noticed your eyes were kinda puffy. You ain't coming down with something, are you?"

Gramps used to say most folks don't notice much beyond the tips of their noses. But then, I thought, most folks haven't gone through what Billy has—having your mama there one day and gone the next.

"I'm just tired," I said. "But thanks for asking."

"Don't mention it." He reached for a fire ball, handing me one, too. The spicy cinnamon aroma filled the night air, making it seem a tad warmer.

"Wendy's birthday's Sunday," I told Billy. "I'm having a party. Think you'd be interested in coming?"

Billy rolled the fire ball from one cheek to the other. "Who else you inviting?"

"Anna Marie Armstrong and Connie Talbot."

He made a sour face. "All girls?"

"You said girls aren't all that bad."

"I meant *some* girls ain't." It was hard to tell if Billy was blushing or if his face was just red from the cold. "Let me think about it, okay?"

I elbowed his side. "Whaddaya say we flip a coin? Heads, you come to the party. Tails, you get to stay home." I felt in my pockets, but they were empty.

"Hang on," Billy said. He leaned sideways and dug in his pocket. He held out a coin, balanced it on his thumbnail, and flipped it high in the air. Then I caught it, slapping it onto the backside of my hand. "Well?" Billy said, trying to peek.

I let him look.

"Aw, nerts!" He swatted his knee. "I've gotta eat cake with the Breck Girls."

I squinted at the coin, holding it up to the porch light. "Hey," I said, "this is a wheat penny. A *silver* wheat penny."

"Yeah. I collect them." He reached in his pocket, drawing out several more.

My mouth dropped open. He had a dozen, at least.

"Wheat pennies were only made of silver for one year—" Billy started.

"In 1943," I blurted out, " 'cause we needed the copper for World War II."

"For the soldiers' ammunition," Billy added, excited. "Then, in 1958—"

"They stopped making wheat pennies altogether," I finished.

Our eyes met. This time we both blushed.

Billy shoved the coins in his pocket. Except for the penny he'd flipped. "Do me a favor and take this one," he said. "Quick, 'fore it gets me in any more trouble."

I reached for the coin, smiling. "Sure. Glad to help."

Billy stood, tugging his mask into place. "I better catch up with Dinky and Elmer 'fore they get lost. If brains were dynamite, they couldn't blow their noses."

"See you Sunday," I called.

Billy moaned, walking away.

Inside our mobile home, the president's face filled the TV screen. "Where's Daniel Boone?" I asked.

"President Johnson's just called an end to the bombing of North Vietnam."

"Does that mean the war's over?" I asked, hopeful.

"Not quite," Gram answered. "But it's a step in the right direction."

I started toward my room with the penny Billy'd given me. As I did, I remembered Madame Paulina's prediction for my future—the friend who would cry a lot, and the boy who would like me. And the penny, the wheat penny . . .

"Holy moly," I mumbled, placing the coin on my dresser—right beside my picture of Gramps. And, as I did, I swear, his smile grew a tiny bit wider.

Second Chances

The next morning, Wendy's hair was completely straight, pulled back in a long, silky ponytail. She was wearing knee socks instead of tights and penny loafers instead of patent leather. "How'd last night go?" I asked her.

"It was eerie without my mother there," Wendy answered. "But Daddy and I talked more in one night than we ever have."

"What'd you talk about?"

"About what it was like being afraid of my own mother, keeping what she did a secret, feeling like I couldn't tell him. I didn't realize how terrible everything had become until I heard myself talking." We started across the playground. "Daddy asked me what I wished for. He said it didn't matter if it could come true or not. In the business world, you focus on your next goal."

"So what did you tell him?"

"I told him I wanted to stop taking dance classes."

I felt like somebody'd dropped a bowling ball on my toes. "But you're so talented! And you've got a great chance of winning the state twirling competi—"

"Stop!" Wendy interrupted. "You sound like my mother."

My stomach sank. "Oh, Wendy, I'm sorry. I—"

"The point is, the competitions and the recitals are what Mother wanted for me. Maybe I managed to convince myself they were important to me. But, deep in my heart, I knew they weren't."

I paused, letting Wendy's words soak in. I thought of how I felt when Gram bought me dresses I hated. And how my insides boiled every time Anna Marie insisted on painting my fingernails. "What *do* you want?" I said.

Wendy smiled. "Don't laugh."

"Promise."

"I'd like to do normal things. You know—play dominoes and do paint-by-number sets and watch Saturday morning cartoons. Regular stuff."

Suddenly, Wendy seemed like any other sixth-grader at Lakeville Grammar School. And it occurred to me, that was exactly what she hoped for. She was tired of being the center of attention.

Across the playground, Anna Marie and Connie ambled toward the bike rack. "Come on," I said. "Let's go invite them to your party."

I collected the mail on the way home. There was a postcard from Trudy, inviting Gram to a Tupperware party, and a letter from Bailey, as well. I unfolded the single sheet.

> *Dear Delores,* she wrote.
> *Mr. Crumb retired so we have a new art*
> *teacher, Miss Davis. She likes my drawings and*
> *calls me "prolific," which means I am "very creative*
> *and very productive."**
> *The Beaver Creek Frog Jumping Contest was*
> *last weekend. Becky Montgomery refused to go with*
> *me because she says frogs are gross and handling*
> *them is even grosser. And you already know Mary*
> *Stingpratt's feelings on the topic. (Remember when*
> *we used to call her Mary Stinkypants?) Anyway, I*
> *named my toad Delores so it would feel like you*
> *were with me, same as every other year. And guess*
> *what? Delores and I won first place! My picture*
> *was on the front page of the* Weekly Herald. *I'm*
> *sending you a copy. Sorry I don't look so great. I got*
> *a rash from the lipstick Becky's mother gave me*

*and I had to stop wearing it. Not that I mind,
really. Pink never was my color.*

*Well, I've got to go now. Mama's napping, so I
have a few minutes to myself. I'm going to enter the
Draw Sparky contest and maybe win a scholarship
to art school!*

Sincerely,

Bailey

**Miss Davis's exact words
P.S. I miss you!*

Tears pricked my eyes, and a fat lump formed in my throat.

I would've expected my face to behave a little differently. After all, I'd just gotten word that Becky Montgomery wasn't the perfect friend Bailey had imagined her to be. But instead of filling with joy, I felt a bone-deep sadness for Bailey.

Carefully, I unfolded her newspaper clipping. A FIRST PLACE ribbon was pinned to Bailey's T-shirt and she smiled widely, hugging Delores to her freckled cheek. I could see the lingering rash that circled her lips. And I could see her eyes shining bright as Fourth of July fireworks. But, mostly, I could see the *real* Bailey Parncutt again.

Wendy's Party

I was setting the table with plates and party hats when Wendy arrived. She was wearing denim pants and an emerald green sweater that matched the color of her eyes. Her hair was still poker-straight. "Happy Birthday!" I said, handing her my present.

"Shouldn't I save it for later?" she asked.

"No, I want you to open it now."

Wendy peeled the paper away, smiling at the paint-by-number dogs.

"I thought they'd go nice in your room. You can tell Bruce I painted his portrait."

She hugged the paintings and thanked me. Sitting at the kitchen table, Wendy said, "My dad gave me his gift this morning."

"Oh, yeah? What was it?"

"A small notebook with a pen to match. He wants me to write down all the things I never got the chance to do because I was busy taking lessons and performing and competing. Every day after I get home from school, we'll try something new on my list. I alphabetized it on the way here."

"That's great." I smiled. "What have you got for A?"

"Actually, I couldn't think of any As. But I have three Bs. Today after the party Daddy's taking me to Sears and Roebuck to pick out a *bicycle*. My mother would never let me have one—you know, because of her accident."

I pictured Wendy choosing a bike to match Anna Marie's and Connie's Schwinns, and my heart sank.

"Tomorrow," she continued, "we're going *bowling* at Lakeville Lanes."

"What's the third B?" I asked, trying hard to mask my disappointment.

"The *third* B is actually the *first* B because it comes before bicycle and bowling." Wendy fidgeted with the cuff on her sleeve. I thought of something she'd told me at the county fair—about being shy but learning to cover it up. For the first time, I could see her shyness showing. "I was, um, hoping," Wendy began, "*you* could help me with the first B, by agreeing to be my *best friend*."

Bailey's face flashed in front of me. I wondered if I'd be betraying her by saying yes to Wendy, especially after I'd been such a poor sport over her making new friends. But then I thought—both Bailey's and my life had changed, and they would continue to change. And saying no to Wendy wouldn't chase that change away. Nothing would.

"Sure," I answered quietly, "I'd like being best friends with you."

A knock came at the door. Billy was there, holding out a small box wrapped in the Sunday comics. "This is for you," he told Wendy. "Sorry, it ain't much."

She peeled back the paper and smiled. "Cracker Jacks! Thank you, Billy."

He grinned. "Don't mention it."

Anna Marie and Connie arrived next. They breezed through the door carrying presents, calling "Happy Birthday!" in unison.

When Anna Marie noticed Billy, she hurried to my side, whispering, "Why is *he* here?"

"Because," I whispered back, "I invited him."

"Dee-Dee," Connie said, changing the subject, "your trailer's much larger than I expected."

"That's because it's a double-wide," I told her, reaching for the Kool-Aid pitcher and filling a tall glass for everyone. "And I prefer to call it a *mobile home*."

Anna Marie rolled her eyes and sat down. "Wendy," she said, "I'm curious. Why isn't your mother throwing your birthday party?"

Wendy twirled a lock of hair around her finger.

"Maybe you should tell her," I said.

Anna Marie leaned forward on her elbows. "Tell me what?"

Wendy glanced at me, then back at Anna Marie. "My mother's staying at my aunt's house."

"When is she coming back?" Connie asked.

Wendy nibbled her lip. "I'm not sure that she is."

"Why not?" Anna Marie wanted to know.

"Anna Marie," Connie said gently, "that's a very personal question."

"Which Dee-Dee obviously knows the answer to," she snapped.

Billy scratched his ear. "Uh, maybe I should take a walk or something."

Wendy turned to face him. "Don't go, Billy." She rolled and unrolled the edge of Gram's checkered tablecloth. "Eventually, all of you will find out what happened. . . . I'd rather you hear it from me." She drew a long, slow breath. "My parents are separating. They decided it would be best . . . under the circumstances."

"What circumstances?" Anna Marie asked.

I reached for Wendy's hand under the table. She grabbed on, squeezing.

"My mother loses her temper and she . . . she hits me. Once she shoved me so hard I hit my head and had to go to the hospital for stitches." Wendy held her bangs up, pointing to a small scar above her eyebrow.

"I remember that," Connie said. "You said you fell out of a tree."

Wendy shook her head. "I've never climbed a tree."

Everyone was silent.

"How come you never told us?" Connie asked.

"I was afraid to. Afraid what my mother would do if she found out." Wendy hesitated. "Afraid what *you* would do."

"What we would do?" Connie repeated.

"Yes. You might stop liking me."

"We wouldn't think that," Connie said. "Right, Anna Marie?"

Anna Marie just sat there.

"It doesn't matter," Wendy said. "I've learned that *real* friends stick with you no matter what." She looked at me, straight on. "Right, Itch?"

My face burned hot as a Florida sidewalk.

"Itch?" Anna Marie sneered. "Who's Itch?"

The heat climbed down my neck, across my chest. "Don't," I said, "please—"

Wendy turned to face me. "Itch is what your grandmother calls you. And I like your grandmother. And I like Itch, too. It fits you, better than Dee-Dee. So, *Itch*"—she brushed her hands together, like she was clapping away what was left of a dirty job—"I think I'd like to open the rest of my presents."

Wendy unwrapped Connie's gift—a record case filled with several 45s by Diana Ross and the Supremes. I smiled, recalling our sidewalk performance.

Anna Marie's present was last. "Wait a second," she said, fumbling in her sweater pocket. "I want to see Wendy's face when she opens this." She unfolded the glasses I'd noticed in her lunchbox some time ago. When she slipped them on, her eyes looked twice their size. She cleared her throat and said, "I'm well aware of the fact that I look ridiculous, so there's absolutely no need to comment. As soon as I turn thirteen, I'm getting contact lenses. Now . . ." Anna Marie patted her gift. "Take your time unwrapping this. It's fragile."

Wendy eased the paper loose. Inside a large see-through case stood an elegant porcelain doll with perfect blond ringlets and a red velvet dress. Her patent-leather shoes were white enough to outshine the moon. "She's beautiful," Wendy said.

"She reminds me of you," Anna Marie said, giving Wendy a quick once-over. "When you curl your hair and wear pretty dresses, that is."

After twisting the lid off, Wendy reached her hand inside the clear tube.

"What are you doing?" Anna Marie asked. "She's supposed to stay in her display case."

Wendy cupped the doll's head, gently sliding her out. "I'm being careful."

Anna Marie shook her head.

Wendy held the doll to her ear, just like she'd done with Bruce the first time I visited her. "*Pssst—Pssst—Pssst,*" the doll fake-whispered. Wendy listened, nodding.

"What'd she tell you?" I asked, playing along.

Wendy bent the doll's legs so she could sit on the table. "She said she doesn't give a crap about her dress *or* her curls. She'd much rather join the party."

Later, after Billy and Anna Marie and Connie had gone home, Gram handed Wendy a small gift-wrapped box. Wendy opened the lid and held up a set of hair clips I'd seen on display at the Cut-n-Curl. I was happy those flowery barrettes were for her, not me. Wendy grinned up at Gram. "Thank you, Mrs. Colchester. They're very pretty."

"Want me to put 'em in for you?" Gram winked. "I'm a licensed cosmetologist."

"Yes, please."

Gram reached to smooth Wendy's hair back. "You've got some serious tangles," she said. "Have a seat and I'll brush them out for you."

Gram separated Wendy's hair into strands, patiently freeing the knots.

Wendy closed her eyes, looking so relaxed I thought she might have dozed off.

Signs

After we arrived home from church the next morning, Gram served my favorite Sunday brunch—biscuits and gravy with fried eggs and corned-beef hash. As we were clearing the table, the phone rang. I guessed from Gram's half of the conversation that it was Mr. Maxwell on the other end. Before hanging up, she said, "Tuesday at nine will be fine."

I was relieved he hadn't chosen Monday—we had the day off school so our teachers could attend a special workshop. By *Tuesday* at nine, I'd be back at my desk, spared the sight of a stranger driving off in Gramps's Bel Air.

Gram returned to the sink, drying the dishes I'd washed. When she was finished, she said, "Come with me."

I followed her down the hall to the tiny third bedroom. A school dress, freshly pressed, hung on a hook beside the ironing board. The lid on Gram's phonograph was propped open, which was nothing peculiar. Gram often played a record while she ironed. But as I stepped closer, I saw it wasn't a Perry Como album, or any other, balanced beneath the phonograph arm. It was a small 45.

Gram said, "I washed our dresser scarves a few days back, and I found something underneath yours." She stared down at the turntable. "A record called 'Yesterday.' That something you bought?"

Gram's brunch churned in my stomach. "Yes, ma'am, but I can explain, I—"

"Why'd you feel you had to hide it?" she asked.

"'Cause I know how you feel about rock 'n' roll bands. And about people wasting money on foolish notions like—"

Gram shushed me. She turned a dial and my 45 dropped onto the turntable. The needle shimmied in the groove, and the sad, sweet melody filled the small room. Goose pimples covered my arms.

When the song ended, Gram said, "Ain't at all like the noise Ruby Lee used to listen to. Not that I'm surprised. You and your mama are different as night and day. Don't get me wrong, you both got a fire burning inside you—I saw yours at Wendy's the other night—but you put yours to good use. Your mama's fire burned wild."

Gram removed my 45, sliding it gently into its sleeve. Handing it to me, she said, "Everybody's got a yesterday they yearn for. But we've got today, too, Lord willing. And that's where He intends us to live."

"Yes, ma'am," I said, too confused to say much else.

Gram walked to the window and parted the curtain. "The night your mama left, your grandpa was out playing cards with some cronies. You were in your high chair, and I was feeding you strained peaches. Ruby Lee was gussying up for a date with some boy she'd met at the Texaco station. She'd had a birthday the week before—her nineteenth— and the transistor radio she'd finagled your grandpa into buying her was blasting away. I'd already told her twice to turn it down, but she didn't. She danced into the kitchen, holding the radio to her ear. When her favorite Buddy Holly song came on, she turned the volume up, higher still. Kissing the top of your head, she shouted over the ruckus, 'Mama, that's what I should've named my baby girl—Peggy Sue, just like the song.' I stomped over, grabbing that dad-blasted thing clean out of her hand. I clicked it off and said, 'Ruby Lee, you're a mama now. You'd best start behaving like one!'" Gram fiddled with the fringe on the curtain. "Ruby Lee never came home. Five days later, she mailed us a postcard from the Grand Canyon."

"Gram," I said, softly, "what's this got to do with my record?"

"I believe the Lord gives us signs," she said, turning to face me. "When I found that record underneath your dresser scarf, I believe He was telling me, *Eunice Colchester, you've got a second chance here. Learn from your mistakes. Bend a little more with Delores than you did with Ruby Lee—*"

"Gram . . . what are you saying?"

"I'm saying you can use my phonograph anytime you want." She touched my shoulder as she walked past. "Just be careful with the needle. Those things ain't cheap. If you break it, I'm docking your allowance."

I received a sign of my own that night. Although I don't rightly know where it came from—from God or Gramps or some quiet place inside me.

At midnight, I was still wide awake. Gram's slippers scuffed past my room, and I rolled close to the wall, listening to the sounds next door—hangers scraping the closet rod, dresser drawers opening and closing, a clock getting wound, a lamp clicking off. *Gram sounds,* I told myself, and the thought seemed suddenly soothing.

When I heard her snoring lightly, I rose quietly, slipping on my sneakers. I buttoned my coat over my pajamas and crept outside.

The air was so cold I could feel my nose hairs freeze. I tiptoed across the driveway and into the field across the way. An owl hooted, and I wondered if it was the same one I'd heard the night we returned from Wendy's.

I glanced back at our trailer, a dark rectangle lit by a single kitchen nightlight. Beyond it, just past the edge of our lot, I saw a tree I'd never noticed before. A tall bony-looking tree that had dropped nearly all of its leaves. In Florida, most of the foliage hangs on year-round, so I wasn't used to naked branches. There was something pretty about the plainness—the black silhouette poised against the star-spattered sky.

My heart fluttered.

The tree spoke to me. *I've got deep roots*, it said. *And strong arms.*

I knew right away what it was telling me.

Trip to Kemp's

That next morning, after Gram left for the Cut-n-Curl, I stuffed my allowance in my pocket, zipped on my jacket, and took off for downtown Lakeville. The stores had changed their window decorations. Jack-o'-lanterns and bats were replaced by Pilgrims and turkeys. A few places had already strung their Christmas lights.

A bell jingled inside Kemp's Hardware, announcing me. "Can I help you?" a man asked. His bald head reminded me of Brother Thompson's—right down to the single flap of hair that spanned his two ears. When the wind blew, Brother Thompson's flap would clap back and forth.

"I'd like to buy some rope," I told the man.

After he helped me find the thickness I needed, I described the slab of wood I was scouting for. He winked and said, "I've got just the scrap in my throwaways."

The board he showed me was perfect. "Could you by any chance drill two holes in it for me?" I asked. I tapped the spots where I needed them.

"No problem," he said, starting toward the back of the store.

I wandered the aisles, peering inside the bins. "Adaptor plate . . . receptacle . . . toggle switch . . . ," I repeated, savoring the sounds of each.

I recognized a familiar smell. A Gramps smell. I heard someone behind me and turned, half expecting to see him standing there.

Instead I was face-to-face with Billy. He rocked from one foot to the other, grinning. "Hey, Delores."

"Hey, Billy." I grinned, too. Then I sniffed. "Are you wearing hair tonic?"

"Yeah. My brother Ernie put it on for me." His lip curled. "Do I look okay?"

"Yeah, you do. And you smell nice."

Billy blushed. "Thanks."

"Whatcha doing here?" I asked him.

"Ernie's trying to fix the kitchen sink." Billy fished a paper out of his pocket. He stared down at the scribbling. "He needs plumber's putty and a basin wrench."

"I saw 'em over here," I said, leading the way toward the next aisle.

Billy followed me, whistling.

The man returned with my wood. I paid for the rope and Billy paid for his plumbing parts. He held the door open and we stepped outside.

The sky had grayed. A strange odor hung in the air.

Billy glanced at my bag. "Whatcha doing with those things?"

"Stop by later. I'll show you."

I stared up at the bare-branched tree.

Using Gramps's Swiss army knife, I cut the rope in half. I climbed the tree to the second branch. Scooting to the center of the limb, I tied both ends in place. Then I jumped down. The ropes dangled in front of me.

Bike tires crunched across our driveway and I looked up. Billy started toward me, blowing on his hands to warm them. "You making a swing?" he asked.

"How'd you get so dern smart?" I said, playing-like.

Billy pretend-swatted my arm.

I reached for the wood plank. Billy slipped one rope through a hole, and I threaded the second. When we'd finished double-knotting the ends, Billy said, "Hop on, I'll give you a push."

I lowered my behind on the wood plank and closed my fingers around the rope. A familiar comfort washed over me.

Billy pushed on the seat, lifting it higher and higher, till his arms stretched as far as they would go. Then he ducked underneath, releasing me.

My stomach lurched as the swing dropped.

Back and forth, I swooped. As I closed my eyes and pumped my legs, I could feel my whole face smiling. A bursting-out-of-my-socks smile that I could barely contain.

When I opened my eyes, white flakes fluttered before them. "Holy moly," I shouted, "it's *snow!*" I dragged my feet to slow the swing and jumped off, landing square on both heels. I held my arms out and tipped my head back, staring upward into the kaleidoscope of whirling white. The cool flakes melted on my cheeks. They perched on the tips of my eyelashes. I stuck my tongue out, tasting them.

Billy scratched his head. "Don't take this the wrong way, um, but you're acting like you ain't ever seen snow before."

"That's 'cause I haven't!" I yelled.

Bel Air Blues

As much as I hated the thought, I knew I had to say my good-byes to the Bel Air. By afternoon it was coated with several inches of snow. I opened the passenger door and slid into the front seat. My teeth chattered as I gathered my coat closer, hugging myself.

I stared over at Gramps's empty seat. And as I did, Gram's gloved hand appeared, wiping snow off the driver's-side window. Soon her face appeared in the glass, too. She waved, then pointed at Gramps's seat—which I guessed was her way of asking to join me. I would've preferred to be alone. Still, I nodded.

"Brrr," Gram said. She dropped down, wiggling her legs beneath the steering wheel, pulling the door closed behind her. She was still dressed in her work clothes. Plus she was wearing a brand-new pair of winter boots. "What are you doin' out here?"

I contemplated fibbing, but decided I'd tell her the truth. "Saying good-bye," I answered, and my voice broke. I coughed, hoping to cover the sound.

"No sense freezing while you do," Gram said. She reached in her pocket and pulled out the car key. She turned it in the ignition and Gramps's car purred like a tomcat getting his ears scratched. She fiddled with this button and that, finally finding the lever for the heat. "Where's the thingamajig for the wipers, Delores?"

I pointed at the wiper control. "Actually, you can go back to calling me Itch."

"Itch," she repeated, turning the wand. The blades went *Whap! Whap! Whap!* superfast. Gram jumped and we both laughed.

I reached over, adjusting the speed. The wipers clapped calmly, side to side.

Slowly, the heat warmed the car. The snow melted from the windows, and the plump flakes danced all around us. It was like being sealed inside a snow globe.

"You mind?" I asked, pointing to the radio.

"Be my guest," Gram answered.

I turned the dial and Frank Sinatra's voice leapt from the dashboard, singing "Someone to Watch over Me."

Gram rested her head back. "Your grandpa used to sing this song to me, way back when we were first dating. He said I was his someone."

I tried to imagine Gram as a young woman, being swept off her feet by Gramps, but I couldn't.

"All those nights you and your grandpa used to sit in this car after supper," Gram said, "what in tarnation were you doing?"

I shrugged. "Just listening to the grass grow."

"Your grandpa's words?"

I nodded. "We'd listen to the radio, too. Most nights he'd smoke a cigar. We'd talk."

"About what?" Gram asked.

"About anything. Sometimes I'd ask him about Mama. I know you didn't like discussing her, but Gramps didn't mind." I stared into the distance, noticing how the snow made the pine trees look lacy. "I know Mama's running off was wrong," I continued. "But she's still my mama, and I like finding things out about her and if any of her rubbed off on me."

Gram smiled. "That day at the county fair talent show, you sounded just like her. That word you used . . . ebber . . . ebbi . . ."

I smiled, too. "Ebullient."

"That's it!" She chuckled. "Ruby Lee was always trying

out new words, looking for ways to slip 'em into conversation. Half the time I didn't know what the devil she was talking about." Gram reached into her pocket for her wallet, turning to a black-and-white photograph. "Here's my favorite picture of her, taken when she was your age."

All the pictures I'd seen of Mama made her look glamorous. Not this one, though. An ordinary-looking girl with short, flyaway hair was dressed in overalls rolled up to her knees and a striped T-shirt underneath. I could see myself in her. Plus I recognized the tree she sat beneath—the same one Gramps hung my Thinking Swing from. "What's she doing?" I asked, studying the notebook on her lap.

"Writing. She loved making up stories. 'Cept she got bored doing anything for more than a few minutes. So none of her stories had endings."

"Do you think Mama will ever try to find us?" I asked Gram.

"I doubt it," she answered sadly. "That'd be too much like finishing a story."

Enigma

In the morning I dressed for school, then poured myself a bowl of Lucky Charms, groaning and moaning as I ate.

When I stood to put my bowl in the sink, Gram

appeared, dressed to the nines. She paused in front of the mirror beside the coat hook, pinching her cheeks to redden them. I glanced down at her feet. She was wearing her special-occasion pumps with the medium heel. I hadn't seen those since Opal and Ed Purdy's daughter's wedding. "Gram," I said, "why are you dressed like that?"

"I've got an appointment downtown before work."

"But what happened to your appointment with Mr. Maxwell?" I asked, confused.

Gram glanced at the clock. "I canceled it."

"So . . . when is Mr. Maxwell coming?"

Gram reached for a hat and adjusted it on her head. "Give me your honest opinion. Is this hat all right, or does it make me look like an old lady?"

Before I could answer, I heard a car out front. "That'll be my ride," Gram said, taking her coat off the hook. She crossed the room, leaned forward, and kissed the top of my head. "That's how I used to kiss Ruby Lee good night. She couldn't stand anybody touching her face." Gram waved her hand. "Strange child."

The car horn tooted.

I stepped to the door, looking out. "Gram, there's a taxicab parked in our driveway."

"Oh, he ain't parked, he's idling. You can bet his meter's running. If you hurry, I'll have him drop you off at school." She slipped on her best Sunday gloves.

I was perplexed as all get-out. "Gram, *please*, tell me what's going on."

Finally, she turned, giving me her full attention. "I enjoyed sitting in your gramps's car talking with you, Delores—"

"Itch," I reminded her.

"Itch," she repeated. "And I reckon I'd fancy doing it again. In the summer we could put the convertible top down, just like you and Orville used to."

"But you—" I started, confused.

"'Course a car can't just sit there," she continued. "The tires'll rot, and mice'll take up residence in the carburetor and chew through the dang hoses, so—"

"How'd you *know* that?"

Gram grabbed her handbag off the counter. "I've learned a few things, too." She stepped to the door, holding it open. The sky glowed behind her, like a curtain on a turquoise stage. If Gramps were there, he'd have said Gram looked *fetching.*

"I've got an appointment at the license bureau at nine this morning," she told me, "to take my written exam. After I pass that, I'll get behind the wheel and take the real test." Gram elbowed my side. "You seen me in action. Think they're ready for me?"

My mouth fell open. "Are you saying you're getting a driver's license?" I glanced toward the driveway. "To drive Gramps's car?"

I didn't wait for Gram's answer. I dove at her, wrapping my arms around her middle, hugging her for all I was worth.

Gram stepped back and smoothed her coat. Then she handed me my lunchbox and milk money and waved her arm toward the open road. "After you," she said.

That day at lunch, Wendy shared stories inspired by her list—the wayward gutter balls in her first bowling attempt, the embarrassment of being the only twelve-year-old in Lakeville with training wheels because she'd never ridden a bicycle. My favorite story, though, was when Mr. Parish took Wendy to the pound to pick up her new dog, Lucy. Wendy passed around Polaroids of a golden-haired, floppy-eared mutt. "You'll get to meet her soon," she told us.

"Oh, I'm *sure*," Anna Marie said, rolling her eyes, which bugged out behind her glasses.

"Be patient," Wendy told her. "It'll happen when I get to the *L*s."

Connie scrunched her nose. "Because Lucy starts with an *L*?"

"No," Wendy answered. "Because then I'll have a lavender room."

Everyone smiled except Wendy. Her expression changed like a sudden shift in the weather.

"What's wrong?" I said.

"Sometimes I miss her," Wendy mumbled.

"Lucy?" Connie asked.

"No. My mother."

"But, Wendy"—Anna Marie glanced over both shoulders, making sure no one was listening—"how can you say that?"

Wendy felt beneath the collar on her dress, drawing out the blue topaz pendant on the silver chain her mother'd given her the day I crouched behind the basement door. "My mother wasn't *always* mean," she said.

Anna Marie shook her head, as if she could never in a million years understand what Wendy had just said. And I thought maybe none of us could, without walking in Wendy's shoes.

But there's one thing I *did* understand—and that's what it's like to feel things that don't make a lick of sense to others. 'Cause I'm sure there are probably plenty of folks who would never understand me—a kid with a heart full of love for a mama who ran off and left her.

"My mother called me last night," Wendy added, "from Aunt Claire's, where she's staying."

Connie leaned forward on her elbows. "Was that the first phone call since she left?"

Wendy nodded.

"What'd you two talk about?" I asked.

"She wanted to know about school. And dance lessons, which I told her I wasn't going to. She started to say something about the state finals but stopped herself. I think she figured out I'm not competing. She also told me, well . . . that she misses me."

There was a long silence. The recess bell rang and kids filed past our table, but we just sat there, waiting for whatever came next. It seemed like the right thing to do.

"My mother said she's done a lot of thinking and

realizes she has a problem," Wendy continued. "She made an appointment to talk with a special doctor who can help her figure out—"

"A psychiatrist?" Anna Marie whispered.

Again, Wendy nodded. "She said she wants to change. And maybe someday come home again."

Except for the four of us, the cafeteria was empty now. Wendy snapped her lunchbox closed, and the tinny sound echoed off the walls.

"Do *you* want your mother to come home?" I asked.

Wendy shrugged. "If the doctor can cure her, I suppose." Her words hung between us, like something small and fragile beating its wings to stay airborne. "But I can't say for sure. And I don't think my father can, either. I hear him at night, crying through the bedroom wall. He feels so guilty about everything."

The cafeteria ladies appeared with their buckets and sponges, wiping the tables around us.

Anna Marie squinted at Wendy. "But why does he feel guilty? What did your father do?"

Wendy answered, "He says he should have noticed what was happening."

A cafeteria lady approached our table, plunking a bucket on the end. We took that as our cue and all stood at once to leave.

As we walked toward the door to the playground, Anna Marie looped her arm through Wendy's. Surprised, I looped mine through Anna Marie's. Then Connie fell into step beside me, doing the same.

When we reached the door, we couldn't fit face-on. So we turned sideways and slid through.

Wendy led the way toward the box of recess gear.

And, like good friends do, we followed her.

When I got home from school, I changed into my dungarees and sweatshirt. I grabbed my coat on the way out the door, attempting to button it as I ran.

I stopped in front of my new Thinking Swing, and stared up at the tree it hung from. A single leaf clung to the highest branch, reminding me of the small hope I'd always clung to, that one day Mama would return. I knew better now.

The sun had dried the seat completely. I clutched the rope, dug my heels in the dirt, and took off.

A squirrel scurried past, then paused for a moment to watch me. He was carrying a nut, and I wondered if he planned on eating it or burying it. But seconds later he was gone, taking my question with him.

Enigma had been one of our vocabulary words that morning, and I'd added it to my Favorite Words list straightaway. An enigma is a mystery, something we can't explain or understand. And both Wendy and I had mamas that fit the bill. Because I would probably never know why mine ran off, any more than Wendy would figure out why her mother made her feel more scared than safe.

Maybe there are some things we never find the answers for, like that third ingredient Gramps said my mama was made of, the one he couldn't quite name. That unanswered question would always whirl through my brain—just like Mama's unfinished stories would float through time without endings.

A strange new ache filled my heart, one that was partly sad and partly happy.

You're growing up, Gramps reminded me.

"I know," I said, closing my eyes, climbing higher and higher and higher.

Amalgamate

Bucolic

Circumspect

Destitute

Digress

Dismal

Ebullient

Enigma

Gabardine

Insipid

Jargon

Lavender

Loquacious

Melancholy

Mirage

Monumental

Nocturne

Omniscient

Perdition

Persnickety

Pristine
Sojourn
Talisman
Umbrage
Unjust
Whip-poor-will
Zinger

Author's Note

Thousands of children and teens are abused or neglected each day in the United States. If you or someone you care about is being abused or neglected, please call the National Child Abuse Hotline at 1-800-4-A-CHILD (1-800-422-4453). You will be directed to push 1 to speak to a hotline counselor. You can also visit their Web site at www.childhelp.org.

Acknowledgments

Thanks to the staff at Henry Holt Books for Young Readers for giving *Itch* a home; my dear friend Steve Blenus for his generous technological support; Trish Duffy, computer goddess, for making house calls on a moment's notice; Nancy Hope Wilson for encouraging *Itch* in its infancy; everyone in my critique groups for helpful and insightful comments; and lastly, mostly, Barbara Burrows, *my* wheat penny, who read every word of every draft and made endless sacrifices so I could write.